Destiny In Flames

Hidden Realms of Silver Lake
Book 4

Vella Day

Destiny In Flames
Copyright © 2018 Vella Day
Print Edition
www.velladay.com
velladayauthor@gmail.com

Cover Art by Jaycee DeLorenzo
Edited by Rebecca Cartee and Carol Adcock-Bezzo

Published in the United States of America
Print book ISBN: 978-1-941835-73-9

One shifter. One mate. No exceptions.

When dragon shifter, Declan Sinclair, was asked to travel to Earth to heal someone, he thought it would be an easy in—easy out affair. Boy had he been wrong. Not the healing part, but what happened during his one-hour visit: he met Chelsea McKinnon. The bad part? His body had exploded with need like he'd never experienced before, which was wrong on so many levels. Declan already had a mate. Sure she'd died in the line of battle, but everyone was aware of the golden rule: one shifter, one mate, no exceptions. So what the hell was going on?

The moment wolf shifter, Chelsea laid eyes on Declan, she knew the two of them belonged together. She was so convinced they were fated for each other that she gave up her life on Earth and moved to Tarradon. So what if Fate said they couldn't be together. She'd find a way. Too bad the journey wasn't anything like she thought it would be. Instead it was dangerous and challenging, but oh, so hot.

Chapter One

*W*E'RE NOT IN *Kansas anymore, Toto, are we?*

Far from it, her wolf answered, sounding excited.

Chelsea McKinnon wanted to pinch herself. The sudden warmth, the intense stars plastered against the sky's inky backdrop, and the distant rolling hills drew her in like nothing she'd ever experienced before. Wow. Had she really just traveled to another realm in a matter of seconds?

"So?" her brother Finn asked. "How was your first portal experience?"

"I'm still trying to absorb it all. It was almost too easy." She took a step to make sure the ground was real and then glanced over at Finn and his mate. "This place is remarkable. You didn't do it justice when you described it." It was vast. Open. Clean. And best of all, warm—a far cry from Tennessee's chilly winter weather. Chelsea unbuttoned her heavy vest.

Kaleena laughed. "There will be a lot more surprises and experiences in the coming weeks. Speaking of which, are you ready for your first dragon flight? We should get going."

Heart still pounding, Chelsea grinned. "Oh, yeah. I'm so not going to be a wimp like my brother was on his maiden voyage."

Finn laughed. "Don't forget when I first arrived, I didn't know dragons existed."

"I'll give you that." Poor Finn had been blindsided by everything within seconds of his arrival. "How about showing me your big dragon self? You say you're huge but seeing is believing."

Neither he nor his mate had dared to shift when they visited

Earth since they didn't need anyone to freak, especially because few knew that dragons even existed.

Finn glanced over at Kaleena. "Ready, my love?"

"Always."

Both Finn and Kaleena stepped back, and in the blink of an eye, they shifted. It might have been pitch black in the middle of the empty field, but Chelsea's sharp shifter eyes were good enough to make out their huge shapes. Holy shit, they were big. Kaleena's black scales were sprinkled with a light rose color, whereas Finn's were interspersed with dark maroon ones. She couldn't wait to study them in the daylight.

"You're huge."

Her brother approached and held out a claw. He'd already explained how flight worked, so there was no reason to be afraid.

"Should I climb on, or will you pick me up?" she asked, knowing full well her brother couldn't answer.

A second later, she was in his grasp, being swept high into the air. Chelsea grabbed hold of his talon and tried to relax, but she wasn't sure she succeeded. When Finn readjusted her in his claws so that she was facing downward, she pretended she was skydiving—something she loved to do. "This is amazing," Chelsea shouted.

Finn squeezed her briefly to indicate he'd heard. Within minutes, the darkness gave way to the bright lights of the city below, meaning the too short ride was nearing its end. Darn. She wanted it to last longer.

He glided over the city toward its center. The traffic, crowded buildings, and street noise gave the town a very cosmopolitan feel. Then with a light touch, Finn set her down on top of a building, released her, and stepped back.

After he shifted, he smiled. "Like it?"

"I loved it. I can't wait to go again."

Kaleena laughed. "Are you sure you're Finn's twin?"

Finn snarled. "Watch it. I'd like to see Chelsea break into a castle and save you."

Kaleena sashayed over to Finn, threw her arms around his neck, and kissed him. "Don't worry, my love, you'll always be my white knight."

Okay, this was awkward. "Ahem, I'm right here," Chelsea chimed in.

They both cracked up. "Let's get you settled," Finn said.

They headed down one flight of stairs before entering a long, well-lit hall. After taking the elevator down two more floors and walking the length of another hallway, they arrived at Kaleena and Finn's condo.

Finn leaned over and used an eye scanner to open the door. That was cool. Chelsea stepped inside. "Whoa." She glanced over at Finn. "You've come a long way, brother."

Finn grinned. "It's all Kaleena's doing. You know my style—easy bachelor pad."

How true. The upscale condo was lavishly decorated with rich beige leather sofas and artwork she bet cost a mint. One picture was of a waterfall, surrounded by lush greenery. She stepped closer, not sure how it was created. It wasn't painted nor was it a photo printed on canvas.

"It's laser generated," Kaleena said, as if she could read Chelsea's mind. "It's quite a painstaking process and costly, but I had to have it." From the way her skin blushed, she had a personal connection to the area, but Chelsea wasn't going to ask for details.

Kaleena turned and walked across the living room to a small entryway. "Here is the guest room. I took the liberty of buying some clothes for you since your backpack couldn't possibly hold enough for everything you'll need."

Chelsea didn't know what to say. "You didn't have to do that. I was planning on doing a lot of laundry," she said as she joined Kaleena.

Her brother's mate hugged her. "Nonsense. We're family."

"Thank you." Her welcome was overwhelming. From the way Finn was eyeing Kaleena though, he couldn't wait to be alone with his mate. "It's late, so I'll head to bed," Chelsea said. "I can't tell you how much I appreciate you transporting me here."

"We're thrilled to have you," Kaleena said.

Within seconds those two disappeared into their room, and Chelsea went into hers. No surprise, the bedroom looked like a designer had handpicked the green and blue décor. Not only did it have a large bed, there was a desk across from it and a seating area under a window. A guest could get used to this.

Despite being tired, Chelsea needed to shower. Her body still vibrated from the flight.

Her only regret in coming to Tarradon was in not being able to tell her friends where she was headed. Her parents knew, of course, and she'd sure miss talking to them—especially her mom. How long she planned to stay was anyone's guess though. After the funding for the animal shelter was cut from her vet tech's office, Chelsea had been laid off since she'd been the last one hired. Ever since then, she'd been unsettled and figured this was as good a time as ever to see where her twin lived.

You came because you want Declan, and you know it, her wolf said.

Declan Sinclair—the man who had haunted her dreams these past few weeks. She never would have believed that someone from another realm might be her mate. Then again, Finn and Kaleena came from different realms, and they were mates.

Fine. You might be right, she shot back.

This trip would give her a chance to see if she'd only imagined the alluring connection between herself and Declan or if it was real. She'd been around him for only a few minutes when he'd come to Earth to heal Ronan, but the intense draw had been undeniable. Chelsea sure hoped his good looks and that huge, strong body of his hadn't been what had thrown her libido into overdrive.

No, they were mates; she was sure of it.

A KNOCK SOUNDED on her bedroom door. "Chels, are you up?" Finn asked.

Huh? Slowly, she cracked open her eyes, forgetting where she was for an instant. Sunshine, along with the warmth of the blue and green décor, greeted her. Holy shit. She'd slept in—something she rarely did. "Coming."

She slipped out of bed, glad she'd decided on wearing body-covering cotton pajamas instead of her usual T-shirt. The moment she pulled open the door, the scent of eggs and bacon reached her— as did a smile.

"Breakfast is ready."

She rubbed her eyes. "What time is it?"

"Eight thirty, but Kaleena needs to head to work soon," Finn said.

Yikes. It was late. "I'll be right out."

After brushing her teeth and dressing quickly, Chelsea rushed out to the main room. Kaleena was in the kitchen piling scrambled eggs onto three plates. A mound of bacon was already on the table, along with a pot of coffee. Everything looked and smelled divine.

"Have a seat," Kaleena said as she carried over the food.

"This is amazing. Thank you."

Finn smiled. "Kaleena is amazing." His mate practically blushed at his compliment. "What would you like to do today?" Finn asked.

"I don't need to be entertained." She could wander the streets for hours, checking out the area.

"I took off today and tomorrow to show you around," he said, tossing her a fake pout.

"Aw, you are the best brother." Chelsea reached out and squeezed his arm. For the next few minutes, they ate the delicious meal in relative silence. "I can see why you are so enchanted by Tarradon. It's a lot like Earth—eggs, bacon, and even great coffee. What more could anyone want?"

"It is quite similar to Earth, but some things are different— dragons for one," Kaleena said.

Chelsea smiled. "I know, but most are friendly, right?"

The glance Finn and Kaleena shared appeared ominous. "For the most part," she said.

Finn had told her about the dragon shifting Royals who had kidnapped Kaleena. "Every society has its bad element I guess."

"Tell me about it. Ugh," Kaleena said.

Because it seemed to be a touchy subject, Chelsea let it drop. Once they finished breakfast, Finn helped Kaleena clean up, refusing to let Chelsea do anything.

"Do you think I could go for a run today?" Chelsea asked. Her wolf was being rather rambunctious—or rather horny—of late.

"Absolutely. There are numerous trails outside the city that are perfect. Just last week, Kaleena and I flew to this one spot, shifted into our wolf forms, and had a great run."

Kaleena sighed. "It was so freeing to be able to be in my dragon form one minute and then shift into my mate's wolf form the next. I love being in the forest surrounded by trees, rocks, and waterfalls."

"That sounds divine." Just the thought made her pulse slow.

Kaleena washed her hands, grabbed her purse, and then said her goodbyes. "Have fun, you two."

"We will." Finn turned to Chelsea. "Are you ready to see a new world?"

"Absolutely." Other than some US cash that she stuffed in her pants in case she wanted to buy something, she left her purse at the condo. She didn't think carrying a purse while in Finn's grasp would be easy.

"I thought I would take you on a tour of the city first by car, and then we can head on out to the countryside. You'll be able to see more of the area in the daytime."

"Sounds great."

For the next few hours, Finn showed Chelsea where to shop for clothes and food, and then took her to an animal shelter on the outskirts of town. "I can't believe how well they treat their animals here."

Finn chuckled. "Did you think they'd be abused?"

"No. I guess since the workers are shifters, they have a great deal of respect for animals."

"I imagine that's true. Ready for your run?"

"More than ready."

"It will be faster if we take off from here."

"Works for me."

This time when he shifted and held out his claw, she climbed on, ready for the adventure. And Finn did not disappoint. She suspected he was being careful about keeping fairly level to the ground since the sudden altitude shifts might have caused some unwanted consequences. When skydiving, she only went in one direction—down.

From this high up, Chelsea was greeted with a great view of the town. For the most part, the tall buildings and dense population were limited to one area—not sprawled out like so many cities in the States. Compared to Silver Lake, Edendale—the town where Finn lived—was massive though not quite as large as Nashville.

It didn't take long before they were soaring over miles of green countryside. The lush landscape was amazing. While Tennessee was beautiful, the expansive grass areas and rolling hills of the Avonbelle Province made it more romantic. Yes, there were roads, and even an occasional castle, farm, or home, but for the most part, the area was uninhabited—except for the sheep—lots and lots of sheep.

Finn made his descent slowly and landed without jarring her. Once she was on the ground, he shifted back. "It's something to see from up above, isn't it?" he asked.

"It's incredible."

"I'm still amazed by this place. Come on. The trailhead is just up this way."

Once they arrived, Chelsea needed to remove her clothes since after her shift she'd be naked. The last thing she needed was to be escorted back to town in tattered clothes. "It must be nice not to have to change every time you shift," she said.

He'd told her that dragon shifters here were imbued with a magic that allowed them to be dressed in the same clothes after their shift as before.

"Totally, but it was odd at first. Kaleena had to convince me to keep my clothes on." He laughed. "I kind of take it for granted now. Not having to replace shredded clothes is a real plus, especially since I fly from one place to another so often. I span large distances and never would be able to hide my clothes beforehand."

"I have to agree that would be tricky."

Even though Chelsea had changed in front of Finn hundreds of times on Earth before taking a run, she felt a little self-conscious this time. She stepped behind a tree, disrobed, and stashed her clothes at the base. She then shifted into her wolf.

The moment she was in her animal form, the endorphins of freedom surfaced, and she howled. Finn was already in his wolf form when she returned to the trail.

He took off, and Chelsea followed.

The next two hours were exciting and exhilarating but quite tiring. Finn showed her lots of waterfalls, some caves, and endless fields of green. Chelsea finally was no longer able to keep up with her brother and had to slow down.

Finn bayed, though she couldn't guess if he recognized their need to return, or if he was mocking her for being out of shape. Eventually, they made it back to the original tree. After shifting and redressing, she walked back to her brother, her muscles rebelling. "You have endless energy," she said.

He grinned. "It's because I mated with Kaleena. My stamina now is incredible."

She laughed. "Then you'll have no problem flying my limp body home?"

"None whatsoever."

As if he could run for ten more hours, Finn shifted into his dragon form. Being able to choose between being a wolf or a dragon still blew her mind. She must have looked too tired to walk over to him, because he flew to her and lifted her up like she weighed nothing.

On the trip home, Chelsea studied the roads. If she could run every day, she'd be in heaven. Back on Earth, she'd become way too sedentary, causing her animal to be discontent.

They arrived at the car on the other side of the city and drove back to the condo. To her surprise, when they entered his home, Kaleena was speaking with someone on the phone. She smiled and then waved at them. Chelsea didn't realize Finn's mate would be home from work already.

Kaleena disconnected and faced them. "How was your run?" she asked Chelsea.

"Fabulous but tiring."

Finn explained where he'd taken her. For a few seconds, he and Kaleena said nothing, most likely communicating telepathically. Talk about feeling like an outsider.

Finn finally faced her. "My lovely mate has been organizing a welcome party for you tonight."

A shot of joy raced up her spine. "For real? I'd love to meet the rest of the family, especially since I've heard so much about them." She hadn't confessed anything about her desire for Kaleena's brother Declan though. She wanted to talk to him again to make sure he was her mate before breaking the news to everyone. Announcing it would be uncool if it weren't true.

"Good, because the party starts in three hours!"

Three hours! That would barely give her time to rest and then dress. "Has everyone accepted?" Chelsea tried to act as casual as possible.

Kaleena's eyes widened a bit. "Yup. The whole Sinclair family, as well as a few of the Caspians, will be here. Someone has to stay behind and mind the store—or rather mind the mine."

She laughed. "Great!"

At least she hoped it would be great.

Chapter Two

DECLAN PACED THE Sinclair office and stabbed a hand through his hair. "What am I going to do?" He spun around to face his cousin Birk.

"It's only a party. What's the problem?"

"The problem is that when I visited Earth to help heal one of the employees at McKinnon and Associates, I felt this odd attraction to Chelsea."

"So? There have been many women I used to feel attracted to, though none are like my Lily. She's my mate." Birk grinned.

The irony wasn't lost on him. Declan had almost the same conversation with Birk not too long ago, only Birk had been the tormented one that time. "That's the problem. The attraction I felt is the same as I had with Bess." There. He'd said it and then had to shake his head to clear the memory of her death.

"Bess? As in your mate?"

"Yes. There is no other Bess." She was the woman Fate had paired him with and the one Fate had taken away.

"Wow."

"Exactly. Now do you see my dilemma?"

Birk stretched out his legs, acting as if this discussion would be a lengthy one. "How much time did you spend with Chelsea when you were on Earth?"

"A few minutes maybe."

Birk waved a dismissive hand. "You can't possibly be sure what you felt. You were probably drained from all the healing, and your dragon was acting up. Subconsciously, you might have been excited that you were back on Earth where you first met Bess."

A thrill of relief coursed through him. "You might be right."

Birk pointed a finger at him. "Something else to consider—what does Chelsea look like? If she has long black hair like Bess, I can see where the confusion might come in."

If only they did look alike. No, Chelsea was delicate and soft-spoken. She also had the prettiest blue eyes with a hint of freckles sprinkled across the bridge of her nose. "They might both be beautiful, but Chelsea is a blonde." Declan grunted, dropped down onto his chair, and dragged his palms down his face.

"I'm sorry. I didn't mean to drag up that painful topic. I know it sucked when she died. If anything happened to Lily, I don't know what I would do."

Declan sat back up and glanced at the ceiling. "It's been lonely without Bess, but I've managed." His voice hardened on the last few words.

"By spending all your time running the mine? That's not healthy either, you know."

Declan gave him the universal Earth symbol of the finger. He refused to accept what his cousin said was true.

"I still don't see the problem with the party," Birk said. "Stop in, say hi to Finn's sister, and then leave. How hard can that be?"

Clearly, Birk had a short memory about lust and desire. Declan huffed out a laugh, but it didn't contain much cheer. "What if I start to glow or my eyes change colors. How do I explain that to my sister?"

"What are you saying? That would happen only if—"

He didn't need Birk to finish the sentence. "I know, I know. Bess was my mate and can be my only mate. Then how come I feel the same strong sexual pull with Chelsea?"

"Are you sure? Really sure?"

"More than sure. It's actually worse! Fuck."

Birk said nothing for a moment. "Then you do have a real problem." He held up a hand. "Remember, this is Finn's twin sister we're talking about, not some woman you met at a bar."

"I rarely go to bars."

"That's beside the point. You need to be extra cautious around her."

Birk was the master of the obvious. "Don't you think I know that? I'm hoping like hell what you said is true—that I was exhausted from treating her friend. Couple that with the fact I was on Earth where I met Bess, and hopefully, that desire pulsating through my veins was a figment of my imagination."

His cousin nodded. "I bet you're right." He patted his thighs and stood. "See? Problem solved."

"It better be." If it wasn't, he didn't know what he was going to do.

"CHELSEA?" KALEENA KNOCKED on the bedroom door.

"Yes?" She slipped off the magenta colored shirt and grabbed the emerald green one, wondering which one brought out her eye color more.

The door opened. "You're not ready? The guests will be here soon."

Chelsea flopped on the bed. "I can't decide what to wear."

Kaleena's brows pinched. "This is a casual get together. It isn't like your Oscar Awards where what you wear will be photographed and shown to the world."

"I know." She sat up and grabbed the navy blue low-cut top. It would go well with the light-colored jeans—and hopefully emphasize her eyes. "I'm just being silly. I want your parents to like me."

Kaleena laughed. "Trust me, they will. They are very accepting people. Even if you wore a burlap sack, they would like you."

Chelsea smiled. The big question was what would Declan think of her? "Good to know."

Chelsea slipped on the top, stood, and then dragged on her

jeans.

"What's really going on?" Kaleena asked with sudden seriousness.

"What do you mean?"

Kaleena sat down on the bed. "This isn't about my parents, is it?"

Her heart dropped. Was she that transparent? She wanted to confide in Kaleena, but she didn't want her brother's mate to think she was crazy. Keeping her desires to herself however, was making her worry more. "No."

"Then what? You can tell me."

"You know when Declan came to Earth a while back?"

"Yes."

Chelsea sat down on the bed next to Kaleena. "There was something about him that really drew me in—and I mean *really* drew me in."

Kaleena smiled. "Yes. Declan is a healer, and his gentle yet strong side appeals to everyone."

But Chelsea wasn't everyone. "I only saw him for a few minutes, but ever since he returned to Tarradon, I can't keep my mind off him."

Kaleena's eyes darkened. "Chelsea, what are you saying?"

She'd have to tell Kaleena and Finn eventually—or rather Declan might. "I'm sure that Declan is my mate."

She squeezed Chelsea's thigh. "Oh, I'm so sorry."

That wasn't what she expected her to say. "Why are you sorry?"

"Because Declan had a mate. Her name was Bess."

Her heart nearly shattered. There had to be a mistake. "Was?"

"She died in battle."

Poor man. "On Earth, a shifter is paired with only one person. Ever. There are no second chances. Is it the same on Tarradon?" *Please say no.*

Kaleena glanced away. "Yes. Perhaps what you felt was lust. I know Declan is my brother, but even I can tell he's hot."

Chelsea tried not to let her disappointment show. "I guess that was it. I mean, for most of the time he was there, we were in different rooms. I really only saw him for a minute when he walked in with Ophelia—our resident witch—and again when he left."

"I'm sure you're right." Kaleena stood. "Finish getting dressed, and then come out and help me put out the snacks."

"Sure."

As soon as Kaleena stepped out of the bedroom, Chelsea's hands shook. She'd been so sure that she and Declan were mates. How had she been so wrong? Tonight at the party, she would reassess her attraction. Most likely his large size—and the fact he was a dragon—had thrown off her libido.

Cabinet doors opened in the kitchen, indicating she needed to hurry.

AS SOON AS Kaleena's parents arrived, both Jamison and Moira Sinclair greeted her but then stepped away to speak with everyone else. Mr. Sinclair in particular seemed excellent at working a room. One by one, she met most of Kaleena's family and some of her cousins. Chelsea enjoyed every one of them.

The party had been going on for a good hour, and while Chelsea was enjoying herself, part of her was ill at ease waiting for Declan to arrive.

She must have looked a little lost because Mr. Sinclair returned to her side. "I forgot to ask, how was your first dragon flight? Did you enjoy it?"

"It was fantastic. Finn is an excellent flyer." Chelsea grinned, loving how easy it was to talk to him.

"He's a fast learner and an excellent fighter. The Guardians are lucky to have him."

"That's nice to hear." Because Finn and Kaleena never expected her to visit Tarradon, they had told her all about the Guardians and how amazing they were.

While Kaleena's dad was interesting to talk to, she would have enjoyed herself a lot more if Declan had shown up. As much as she wanted to ask Kaleena if her brother was actually going to come, she didn't want to look desperate. It was stupid for her to even think about him, because obviously he wasn't her mate, nor could he ever be. Still...

Chelsea sighed. Lust sure had a way of making her rationalize things. The facts of life aside, Declan was single, and she was single. What harm could a little romp in the hay do? She wanted him, so why not scratch that itch?

"How long do you plan to stay on our wonderful realm?" Jamison Sinclair asked, interrupting her musings.

"I'm not sure. A few weeks maybe? Due to a downsizing at the veterinarian office where I had worked, I was recently laid off, so now I'm footloose and fancy free."

Jamison grimaced. "I'm sorry. That is tough, but I'm happy you took the time to visit. Finn often talks about you."

"We do have a special twin link. The goal for my stay is to make the most of my time off." She smiled, not needing him to feel sorry for her.

Finn eased away from his mate and came over to her. Jamison nodded. "I should make sure my mate isn't stirring up too much trouble. Nice talking to you and welcome to Tarradon."

"Thank you."

Finn placed a hand on her arm. "How's it going?"

"You were right. Kaleena's parents are wonderful, and Tory is a hoot. I think she and I will get along quite famously."

Finn nodded. "I agree. She'll be good for you."

"Good for me, how?"

"I just meant that Tory is the adventurous type. She's fun. Given the loss of your job and all, Tory could brighten your day, so to speak. Not only that, since Tory and Kaleena are twins, you two could talk about the strength of twin links."

"I'd like that." Though what could really brighten her day would be a hot, sweaty affair with Declan Sinclair. Just as that thought crossed her mind, the door behind her creaked and popped open, causing Chelsea's wolf to go wild. Oh, shit. Those vibes. That heat. The pulsing between her legs.

Stay calm, she commanded her wolf.

He is your mate! her wolf said with total confidence—or was it defiance?

No, he's not. He's already had a mate.

"I see Declan finally showed up," Finn said with a grin. Shit, had Kaleena told her brother that she lusted after the man? "Let me introduce you."

Damn. "Great, but let me freshen my drink first." Before he could accuse her of making an excuse, she rushed over to the dining room table where the snacks and drinks were spread out.

While her hearing was sharp enough to listen in on their conversation, she focused her attention elsewhere, not wanting Declan to know how much she wanted him. Already, her nails had sharpened, and when she ran her tongue along her teeth, her canines nearly cut the skin.

Stop it, will you!

I can't help it, her wolf shot back, not sounding sorry in the least.

Her back was to Declan and Finn, but she could feel the strong pull of desire grow by the second.

"Chelsea?" Finn tapped her shoulder.

Every muscle locked, but after a second, she managed to spin around and will her heart to slow. It was Declan. Oh. Holy. Hotness. His short brown hair gave him an air of total confidence, but it was the trimmed scruff on his face that added a look of danger—as in: *come here, and you'll lose your heart to me* kind of danger. If that wasn't enough to heat her body to boiling, his whiskey colored eyes seemed to see straight through her.

"You remember Declan," Finn said, sounding way too amused.

Like she could ever forget that face, that voice, and that body.

"Hi."

It was all she could do to say that one word. Chelsea held out her hand, and when he shook it, a bolt of electricity raced up her spine. What she wouldn't give to be able to block his allure.

Inside, she was seething that Fate was laughing at her, putting this yummy, off limits man in front of her. Her sole purpose in coming to Tarradon was to find her mate. Boy, had she been a fool.

"Nice to see you again," Declan said. His words came out as smooth as water flowing over a damn. Clearly, he was used to having women ogle him.

Finn stepped back. "I'll let you two talk."

What? Talk? She wanted to kill her brother. Chelsea wasn't capable of much other than drooling. To defuse some of her nervousness, she curled the bottom of her shirt and shifted her weight.

"How's Ronan?" Declan asked, his brows pinched in concern.

The breath she'd been holding released. Talking about someone else would help. "His wolf healed him very quickly after you left. He has you to thank for his life."

Declan smiled, and Chelsea was sure she'd never seen anything more inviting, forcing her to inhale to calm her stupid libido.

"I merely added a touch of magic to the healing process. Ophelia did most of the work. Ronan's wolf finished the job." While his tone was upbeat and quite self-deprecating, sadness seemed to fill him.

"I know my cousin Blair was very thankful that you helped him."

"I'm glad."

Declan kept studying her. Was it the blue of her eyes that drew him in? Or was he wondering why a grown woman seemed ill at ease around him?

She could do this. "What do you do here?"

He cocked a brow, probably assuming that either Kaleena or Finn had given her a rundown on every family member. "I oversee the running of the Sinclair and Caspian mines. I have a lot of support, so the job isn't too demanding. And you?"

Interesting. He wasn't the type to yammer on and on about his very important job. "I'm an unemployed vet tech who's a victim of downsizing."

"I'm sorry. Hence the time off to come here?"

"Yes."

"How long do you plan on staying?" His chest expanded as if he was holding his breath.

She couldn't tell if he wanted her to say she'd be gone soon or if she planned to stay indefinitely. Chelsea certainly couldn't say it depended on him. "I'm not sure. I want to learn a bit more about Tarradon. I've only been here one day, but so far it holds a lot of appeal."

"Crap." He patted his pocket. "If you'll excuse me. I just received a text." He pulled out his cell, scanned it, and returned the message. "I'm sorry, but something came up that I have to attend to."

"At seven at night?" she blurted.

He gave her that dazzling smile again. "The mines run twenty-four hours a day."

"Oh."

Chelsea wanted to ask why someone else couldn't handle the emergency, but if Declan stayed, she might make a bigger fool of herself. The man did something to her insides, and she couldn't afford to fall for him. Heartbreak—especially on a different realm—was the last thing she needed.

Chapter Three

DECLAN PRESSED HIS back against the wall of the hallway outside his sister's condo. What the hell was wrong with him? He'd stepped one foot inside the room, and his dragon built an inferno inside him. It didn't matter he told his animal that Chelsea was not his mate—Bess had been—but his horny dragon refused to listen.

He chalked it up to the fact that he had been working non-stop since Bess died three years ago. Women had always interested him, but the moment he met the young college student from Colorado, he never looked at anyone else again—until Chelsea.

Even his dragon had agreed that Bess was his mate. When he'd bitten the human, she'd turned into a dragon shifter—proof they were fated for each other. So why was it happening again?

Birk had to be right. Declan had been so consumed with working the Guardian cases and making sure both mines were run well, that he'd neglected the needs of his inner animal.

Declan pushed off from the wall and headed straight to the staircase. Taking the steps would provide a bit of energy release, so he ran the three flights to the rooftop where he took off for the mine.

The text message had been a total ruse to distance himself from Chelsea. He had to do it. Everything about her excited him. As much as he tried, he hadn't wanted to drown in those eyes that were bluer than the clearest lake, but he couldn't stop himself.

Fuck. Now what was he supposed to do? He could only hope that by working until he dropped, Chelsea's allure would dissipate. There had to be some explanation for the attraction—only he couldn't for the life of him figure it out.

The cool night air and star-filled sky might have helped clear his head, but it had done nothing to rid his body of the intense desire swimming through his veins. Everyone always commented that Declan Sinclair was the epitome of control, and that his easy-going manner conveyed confidence. If anyone saw him now that image would have been shattered.

Once at the mine, he headed inside. Thankfully, no one was there. Declan had thought his cousin Birk would be at his desk, but even he seemed to have finished his work and was now probably out enjoying himself with Lily, the love of his life.

Declan scooted his chair up to his desk and pretended it was a usual Saturday night. He pushed aside all thoughts of what everyone else might be doing and studied this month's revenue.

A half hour later, he found himself staring at the same page. This sucked. Maybe he should embrace his feelings and go out with Chelsea in order to purge her from his system. Most likely, this rush of hormones was his body's way of coming to life again after Bess' death. Hell, he'd been in mourning all these years, and Chelsea had lit the ember in his gut.

He wasn't sure how long she'd be here, but he'd give her a few days and then conveniently bump into her. Happy with his newfound solution, he refocused on the books.

BY DAY THREE, Chelsea was beside herself. She had hoped she'd bump into Declan or at the very least, he would have asked her brother for her phone number but no such luck. Finn had purchased a new cell for her so she'd be connected, but perhaps Declan didn't think she'd have one.

Clearly, she was the only one who had been affected by the sexual attraction. Damn. One-way affairs were the worst kind of emotional rollercoaster. However, she wasn't giving up.

Finn had given her keys to his car since he preferred to fly everywhere. For the last two mornings, she'd woken up long after both Kaleena and Finn had left for work. After eating, Chelsea headed out to go for a run at the place Finn had first taken her to. Chelsea was the first to admit that exploring Tarradon while in her wolf form had been fantastic and exhilarating.

She would return around lunchtime, chow down last night's leftovers, and then wait for either Kaleena or Finn to return home. Not being able to communicate with anyone on Earth was the biggest downer, but it was a small price to pay for being able to experience this amazing world. Now however, it was time to make some changes.

Chelsea wanted to stay here—at least until she had her fill of Declan Sinclair. After that, Earth might hold more appeal. To do that however, she needed money, which meant a job. As wonderful as this condo was, hearing her brother and his mate go at it every night for hours just wasn't her thing. A new place to live was also needed. The question that plagued her was would someone from Tarradon hire a person from Earth?

To her delight, Finn came home just as she finished lunch. He said he normally did some Guardian stuff in the morning—or goofed off if they didn't need him—and then tended bar four nights a week. That meant he was often free for lunch.

"You look excited about something," he said. "Want to share?"

Finn always could sense her every mood. "I've decided I want to give living on Tarradon a try."

His eyes widened. "Oh, really? Even though Declan is not your mate?"

She tried not to let his words sting. "Yes."

Chelsea certainly wasn't about to tell him that just because they weren't mates didn't mean they couldn't indulge in some hot and heavy kissing, touching, and sheet-twisting sex. Once she became tired of Declan—or Declan of her—she'd consider moving back.

"I thought you said you came here to be with him."

Kaleena had a big mouth. "I never said those words. And even if I did, now that I know Declan had a mate, I plan to just enjoy myself here."

Finn grinned. "Liar. Even after you learned about Declan's mate, you were completely enamored with him at the party."

He was making that up. "Was not."

Her twin laughed. "It doesn't matter. You're here, and that makes me happy—Mom and Dad though, probably not so much."

She slumped. "I do miss them, but I was stuck in a rut back on Earth. Without a job, I felt lost. I'm hoping that being here will give me a new perspective on things."

"What can I do to help?" he asked.

"Do you know of any animal shelters or vets that might be hiring?" They had been to one shelter, but they had a full staff.

"No, but let me ask around. I think Griffin mentioned something about some shelter that recently opened." He pulled out his cell and called Kaleena's cousin. "Hey, Chelsea is planning on staying in Tarradon for a while and is looking for a job as a vet tech or anything to do with animals. Do you know of someone who might be hiring? Uh-huh." He paced while he listened. "Okay, we'll give them a try." He disconnected and faced her. "There is a vet's office on the edge of town that has been looking for someone. Want to check it out?"

"Now?"

"Why not?"

That was too good to be true. "Absolutely. Are we flying or driving?"

Finn chuckled. "Driving. I need the GPS. Besides, landing anywhere close to the city is tricky. Not every place has a rooftop door that leads to a stairwell."

That worked for her. They headed to the parking garage, and she showed him where she'd last parked. Because Finn was used to driving around Edendale, she slipped in the passenger side. He exited the garage and headed east.

"Did you have to save anyone today?" she asked, wanting to take her mind off Declan.

He chuckled. "No. A lot of the Guardian work involves legwork and searching on the Internet. Crime is about the same here as on Earth, though the Tarradons seem to be a bit better at hiding their illegal activities." He looked over at her. "You aren't going to ask if I saw Declan today?"

She'd asked the last two days. "Nope. I'm over him."

"Uh-huh."

She didn't know why she bothered to lie. Chelsea never could keep anything from him.

It didn't take long before they arrived at the veterinarian's office. It was a lot smaller operation than the one she worked at in Silver Lake, and her hopes plummeted. Most vets worked on a shoestring budget, but if Griffin said he heard there was an opening, she wanted to ask.

Once inside, the woman tending the desk looked up and smiled. She was so beautiful that Chelsea was surprised she wasn't doing modeling work. Her nametag read Sabrina, and she looked as exotic as her name. She had long black hair down to the middle of her back and the prettiest ice blue eyes.

"Hello, can I help you?"

"I'm a vet tech who's looking for a job. I heard you were hiring." Chelsea explained about her educational background and experience.

"I'm really sorry. We just filled the spot yesterday." The woman looked genuinely disappointed.

Chelsea looked over at Finn, but he didn't seem all that concerned. "Thanks anyway."

"What about an animal shelter?" Sabrina said as Chelsea turned to leave.

She spun back around. "Do you know of one who is hiring?"

"I do." Sabrina gave them the directions. "Tell Stick I sent you. He's my brother."

Stick? Chelsea wondered how he had earned that nickname. "I

will, thank you."

Once they left, Finn wrapped an arm around Chelsea's shoulder. "If this animal shelter doesn't pan out, I imagine the Sinclair office could use you."

She shook her head. Chelsea couldn't imagine working in close proximity to Declan. That would drive her crazy. Most likely she'd become so distracted that they'd fire her.

This animal shelter was in the opposite direction of the first one and quite far out of town, but as soon as she saw the space for the animals to run, she had a good feeling about it.

A tall, thin man was outside feeding the animals. While they were in pens, the animals looked well fed. The man emptied his bowl, wiped his hands down his pants, and came over to them.

"Welcome. Looking for a pet to adopt?"

As much as she wanted a dog, she needed to establish herself here first. "Actually, I'm looking for a job." She explained how Sabrina had recommended this place.

"I could use some help, but I can't pay you too much."

Chelsea glanced over at Finn. "How much isn't too much?" Finn asked, acting like the protective brother.

"Three hundred Denlars a week."

She wondered what that would be in US dollars. When Finn nodded though, she guessed it was fair. "May I look around first?"

"Sure." He held out his hand. "I don't know where my manners are. I'm Seth Parnell, but everyone calls me Stick." He swiped a hand up and down his thin body to indicate why the nickname fit.

She shook his hand. "Chelsea McKinnon."

"We just got in two tramors. Maybe you'd like to see them."

"What are tramors?"

His brows rose. "Are you from Earth or something?"

He made it sound like a bad thing. "Yes."

Seth nodded. "They're a cross between a wolf and a sintor."

She didn't dare ask what a sintor was. Seth led her to a cage where two mangy animals resided. Both were pacing. As soon as they spotted Seth, they bared their teeth and growled. Okay, that wasn't good.

Chelsea knelt down in front of the cage to study them, and they both calmed. The brown and white spotted one eased toward her, raised his nose in the air, and sniffed. When his tongue lolled out, she smiled and then glanced up at Seth. "He seems sweet enough. May I feed him?"

"Be my guest, but if he attacks, I'm not responsible. I'll get them their food."

As soon as Seth, or rather Stick, left Finn stepped up next to her. "Are you sure you should be near those animals? I've never seen anything like them before. They look mistreated."

"That's why they're here. Don't worry. My charm, or should I say my magical talent, is being able to handle animals."

"Maybe that means you are Wendayan, too. Have you ever had blue sparks shoot off your body when you're...um...sexually excited?"

Where had that comment come from? Her face heated. "No, though I always did wonder about my abilities."

"I inherited great grandmother's ability to dream-walk with Kaleena. Maybe your ability with animals was inherited from her too."

She'd never thought about that. "Could be. If I ever start to glow, I'll let you know."

"There's nothing like seeing sparks jump off your body."

"I won't be seeing them any time soon. I thought they were reserved for when I was with my mate."

"They only showed up on me when I met Kaleena, so maybe that's true."

Before she could comment, Stick returned and handed her a bowl full of food and then unlocked their cage. "Have at them."

Wanting to show him she was good with animals, she bent over and stepped into the cage, knelt down, and placed the food in front of them. Both tramors dove for their meal. Poor things. She hovered her hand over the brown and white spotted one's head and then petted him. The animal seemed to purr.

"I'll be damned," Stick said.

Chelsea inwardly smiled. She stroked the second one's back. When they finished devouring the food, they dropped down onto their haunches, seemingly content.

She grabbed the bowl and backed away from them toward the cage door. Once outside she stood.

"Are you interested in the job?" Seth asked.

"Yes!"

"Great. Can you start tomorrow?"

This was too good to be true. "I sure can."

Now all she had to worry about was whether Finn could lend her his car until she could afford to buy one.

Chapter Four

WHEN DECLAN BREEZED into the office the next morning, Finn glanced up from his desk. "Hey."

No one other than Finn had arrived. Good. Declan wasn't in the mood to be cordial. For every hour that had passed since Chelsea's welcome party, Declan's mood had grown darker.

"Something wrong?" Finn asked, nodding to Declan's face.

Without thinking Declan dragged a hand down his jaw. Shit. He'd been so preoccupied this morning, he hadn't shaved. "I was in a rush."

"Uh, huh." A twinkle sparkled in his eye.

Did Finn know something? Not wanting to deal with him now, Declan headed over to the coffee machine at the back of the room and poured himself a cup. When he returned to his desk, Finn was still staring at him. "I said I was in a rush. There's no crime in that, is there?" Declan asked, not pleased with his gruff response.

"Whoa. Stand down. All I'm saying is that you seem distracted." Finn leaned back in his chair, legs outstretched, with a cat-ate-the-bird look. "You know, ever since Ophelia begged you to return to Earth to help heal Ronan, you've been…withdrawn." Finn sobered. "Is there anything I can do to help?"

Declan waved a hand. "No. I've just been worried about all the fires on the other side of the province." That was lame. Sure, he was concerned, but no lives had been lost. Yet.

"The fires have you worried? I know there have been a rash of them, and several farmers have lost their crops, but I don't see how that is the responsibility of the Guardians, or am I missing something here?"

"Those setting the fires need to be stopped."

Finn's brow rose. "I agree, and I'm happy to help. If you want, I can talk to Josh Gerrard to see if there is something we can do."

If only the arson investigator could solve his problems. "Not yet. If the farmers find out whoever's responsible, and then decide to take things into their own hands, violence could erupt. That's when we'll intervene."

"Is that the only thing that has you upset?"

"Who says I'm upset?"

Finn barked out a laugh. "Really?"

Clearly Chelsea's twin wasn't going to let it go. Hell, even though Declan had confided in Birk, Finn might be able to give him the inside scoop. "Fine. It's your sister."

Finn sat up straighter, all cheer evaporating from his face. "Did she call you or something?"

He wished she had. It might have calmed his libido. Leaving only a few minutes after seeing her at the party had been stupid and quite shortsighted. How did he think he could analyze his feelings in such a short period of time? "That wouldn't have been a problem, though she would have no reason to contact me."

Finn shrugged. "Then what is the issue?"

Declan picked up his coffee cup and blew the steam off the top. "You never met Bess, my mate."

"No, but Kaleena has told me a few details about her. What does this have to do with my sister?"

From the one raised brow, he knew what the problem was. "Everything."

"Spill."

Declan's hand was actually shaking. Providing Finn with details might help. "About six years ago, I was in Colorado brushing up on some mining techniques at the university there when I met Bess Lambert, a human." Declan shook his head. "She was so sweet and innocent, but I knew right then and there that she was my mate."

"I know what you mean. Did she feel the pull too?" Finn leaned forward, his elbows on the desk.

"She was attracted to me but not like I was to her."

"That makes sense since she was a human. Eventually, you told her about being a shifter—a dragon shifter, no less, right?"

Declan nodded. "Yes, and you can imagine my surprise when she said she was okay with it. I tried to impress upon her that being told I was a dragon and actually seeing me as one were two different things." He could still remember the look on her face the first time he shifted. He'd feared she'd shriek, but she actually had jumped with joy.

"Then what happened?"

"Then we did the dating thing for a while. When it came time for me to return to Tarradon, I asked her to come with me."

"Obviously she agreed but wasn't she afraid? I mean learning about shifters had to be a big step for her—as was leaving her life behind."

"You would have thought so. To my delight, she wanted to go, and even said she didn't care what I was. I won't go into detail, but she'd had a stalker in Colorado and feared for her life."

"She was running away?"

"Kind of, but that wasn't what prompted her to say yes—at least I don't want to believe it had been. We loved each other. If I thought Bess was using me as an escape, I wouldn't have taken her with me. Just so you don't think I'm a cad, we didn't mate until several months after we arrived here. I wanted her to understand our culture first."

"Which apparently she did."

Declan nodded. "Good ole Bess. I still can't believe how excited she was when she saw me in my dragon form. She actually wanted to parade me in front of her friends back on Earth—in my animal form, of course."

Finn laughed. "Yeah, that wouldn't have gone over well."

"No."

"Then what happened, if you don't mind me asking?"

Declan's family knew most of the story. He was surprised Kaleena hadn't filled him in. "After Bess and I mated, she embraced her dragon side."

"If Bess hadn't been your fated mate, she wouldn't have been able to become a dragon, right?"

"Right."

Finn waved a hand. "Go on."

Right before Declan left for Tarradon, he'd asked Ophelia about his odd reaction to Chelsea, hoping she'd say that when a mate died, Fate allowed a shifter to take a second one, but the wise woman said she'd never heard of anything like that happening.

"During the time Bess was here, many humans were being mistreated by the Royals. That was before Kaleena killed Prince Rathan. This injustice infuriated her. Bess insisted on being trained to fight, and Thane agreed to take her on. I swear she worked harder than anyone I'd ever seen. Her goal was to be the best—and she was."

"Kaleena told me she was killed in battle. I'm sorry. I'm guessing she was attacked by more than one dragon then?"

"By three dragons to be exact. I was being attacked myself at the time. Once I killed my assailant, I swooped in to help Bess. Two of the three that were attacking her turned and charged me. The one who remained to fight Bess gained the upper hand—or rather the upper claw. Bess was already injured severely when he stabbed her in the heart."

"I'm sorry."

Declan sipped his now cooled coffee, hoping to push aside the horror of that day. "Me, too. Once Bess fell to the ground, the one remaining dragon I was fighting took off. The one who killed Bess seemed to be targeting her."

"Do you know who they were?"

"No. I've looked for them for years but always come up empty-handed."

"Do you know why they attacked Bess or you?"

"No. We were working on several cases at the time, so I never could figure it out. By the time I reached Bess on the ground, she was unconscious from the blood loss. I worked tirelessly on her, pouring all of my magic into her, but it wasn't enough. I've always wondered if I'd called Greer and asked her to help if the two of us could have saved her."

"Declan, don't do this to yourself."

Like he hadn't heard that before. "It's hard not to. I think of Bess every single day—or at least I used to until recently."

"Did something happen to change that?"

"Chelsea happened."

Finn huffed. "I don't understand...or maybe I do."

His pulse shot up. "What do you mean?"

"You first."

That was only fair. "I can't explain it. I've seen your sister, what? Twice for maybe a total of fifteen minutes, yet I feel this attraction to her."

"She likes you too."

Declan couldn't tell by his tone what that meant exactly, but Finn might not know much more than that. "In what way?"

"Shit. I shouldn't have said anything. I mean, she's my sister."

"And this is my sanity here."

Finn held up a hand. "I'll just say that her reason for coming to Tarradon might have been more than just seeing where I live."

Declan didn't want to jump to any conclusions. "Are you saying she came because of me? Did she feel the pull too?" Though that would mean they'd both be miserable when they couldn't mate.

"I suggest you ask her," Finn said.

"Trust me, I plan to."

CHELSEA HAD JUST finished running a comb through her wet hair when the condo's front door opened. Yay! Finn must be home.

Kaleena had called and said she had to work late. Chelsea rushed into the bedroom, tossed on a top, and then stepped into the living room. "Hey," she said. "How did your day go?"

"Good." Finn strode over to the fridge and grabbed a beer. "You want one?"

Her brother didn't drink very often. "Is something wrong?"

"I don't know, but I think we should talk."

That didn't sound good. "Then sure, grab me one."

Finn handed her the drink. "I had a talk with Declan today."

At the mention of his name, her pulse soared, and her stomach churned. "Oh, really. How's he doing?" Chelsea was pleased with her calm delivery.

"He told me how he met his mate and how she died."

Chelsea didn't want to know. "Why did he tell you?"

Finn stepped over the sofa and patted the seat next to him. Chelsea sat and lifted her drink to her lips.

"I think he's conflicted."

"About?"

"His feelings for you."

Good thing she hadn't taken a drink or Finn might be wearing it. "Why would you think that? At the party, we spoke for a few minutes before he was called away. That was a couple of days ago."

Finn held up a palm. "I know. As I said, he's conflicted. He had a mate. Bess was a human he met in Colorado. Long story short, they fell in love—my interpretation of the events—and she came back to Tarradon with him. They mated, and she became quite a powerful dragon shifter fighter."

"I know he already had his one chance at a mate. I've accepted that." Not well, but what choice did she have?

"Three years ago, she was killed in battle, and Declan, the healer, somehow blames himself for not having been able to save her. He thinks if he'd called in Greer, Bess would be here today."

"What does this have to do with me?"

"Declan has spent every day of the last few years thinking about her—until he met you."

That made her laugh. "He doesn't know me."

"I know, but he feels a very strong attraction toward you."

He wasn't helping her cause to cast Declan from her mind. "What are you suggesting? That I ask him out?"

"All I'm saying is that Declan might not be a lost cause. He might not be your mate, but why not enjoy spending time with each other while you're here."

She huffed out a laugh. "And get my heart broken when I leave? No thank you." When she'd changed her mind about a mindless affair she didn't know. Maybe it was before she'd learned that Declan felt some pull toward her. It made him more dangerous.

Finn clasped her hand. "I want to see you happy. Maybe if you're with Declan for a while, you'll see that it isn't meant to be, and you'll be able to move on."

No, he is your mate. When her wolf suddenly interjected, Chelsea tried not to jerk at the intrusion.

"You do have a point, but what if I fall in love with him. Knowing we can never truly be together would do more harm than good."

Finn smiled. "You won't know until you try."

"I'll think about it."

"How about a hug?" Finn asked. It was something he always did when she needed solace. And boy, did she need it now.

Chapter Five

"TO YOUR NEW job!" Tory said, holding up her glass of red wine. Kaleena, Lily, Nessa, and Greer all held up their drinks and then chimed in.

"Thank you for inviting me to happy hour. Having new friends in a strange place really helps me feel at home," Chelsea said.

"Tell us about this new job," Nessa said.

"I've only worked there two days, but it's an animal shelter. The owner, Seth Parnell—nickname Stick—just started the business and only has one other employee—a man by the name of Marty. He's really into animals too. Stick's sister, Sabrina, helps out when she isn't working at the vet's office in town."

"What kind of animals does Marty and this Stick fellow rescue? The usual cats and dogs, or is there anything more exotic?" Nessa asked, sounding excited.

"He has a little of everything." She told them about the two tramors they'd received.

"Ooh, they are mean," Tory said.

"Actually, they were quite sweet, though I had to bribe them with food and some heavy petting before they trusted me." The group looked at her as if she were crazy. "If Finn didn't mention it, I have a *talent* with animals. I'm not a healer like Greer, but I've been known to speed the recovery process of animals. When I'm around them, there is a unique connection between us. I seem to be able to calm animals along with giving them a sense of safety with me."

"You're what the people from Earth call an animal whisperer," Greer said.

"Yes, but it can extend to more than that at times."

"Very cool," Nessa said. "What else is at the shelter?"

"One animal came in today that I have never seen before. It's called a sintor. At first, I thought it was a lynx, but then Marty told me about the breed. It's a rather beautiful animal and very graceful."

Greer stared off for a bit. "That's interesting you mentioned a sintor. A friend of mine was in the jewelry store today to pick up a ring she'd ordered and was quite upset because her pet sintor was missing."

"Is that a common animal around here?" Chelsea asked.

"Quite the opposite," Greer said. "It is rare. She paid thousands upon thousands of Denlars for it."

"Hmm. I'll have to ask Stick where he found the animal. I figured people brought in the animals they no longer wanted, but if a sintor is so expensive, I doubt anyone would just leave it at the shelter."

Greer leaned forward. "You said the animals are well-cared for, right?"

"Yes, they even have space to run."

"You don't find that odd?" This came from Kaleena.

"Not really. I just figured that people on Tarradon respected their animals more than some people do on Earth."

The woman looked at each other. "They mostly do," Kaleena said, "but there are a lot of homeless, abandoned, and abused animals too."

"All of the animals at the shelter appear to be very healthy—except for the two tramors. Hmm."

"Did this Stick guy say if the animals are mostly dropped off, or does he pick them up if they are wandering about without a collar?" Tory asked.

Chelsea shook her head. "He never said, other than Marty finds them." That made her sound so naïve. "It didn't occur to me that anything unlawful might be happening. Greer, maybe your friend can come to the shelter and see if the animal we have is her sintor.

It's possible her pet ran away."

She shook her head. "Marianna said she keeps Toran in a penned area."

"Maybe a dragon shifter swooped her up. We have owls in America who steal cats when they can."

"It's possible."

When the women said nothing more, Chelsea hoped they would let the issue drop. She'd finally found a job that she liked and didn't want to think she was working for some scumbag.

AT WORK THE next day, Chelsea spent a few extra minutes with the sintor, trying to figure out why someone would abandon such a pretty animal. "Are you Toran?" she asked, knowing full well, he probably wouldn't recognize his name.

Wrong. The animal jerked his head. Okay, maybe he did understand her.

"How do you like our new find?" Stick asked. The sound came from right behind her, causing Chelsea to jump.

As calmly as she could, she twisted around. "Yes. I've never seen anything like him before. Where did you get him?"

"Ask Marty. I believe he found him roaming in the countryside and feared something bad might happen to him since he looked lost."

Chelsea had to force a smile. "That's wonderful that he was able to save such a lovely creature." She turned back to the animal and rubbed him behind the ears. "We'll find you a good home, Mr. Sintor."

Stick shuffled off. As soon as he was out of earshot, Chelsea called Greer.

"SinCas Jewelers, how may I help you?" Greer said, sounding so professional.

"Hey, Greer, it's Chelsea," she whispered, not wanting Stick's shifter senses to pick up her conversation. She explained how their new sintor seemed to recognize his name. "The animal could belong to your friend, Marianna. Stick said Marty found him wandering in some field."

"Marianna said the fence was not broken, but I'll let her know. Where is this new shelter?"

Chelsea gave her directions.

"Thanks."

"You bet."

She disconnected. "Who was that?" Stick asked, scaring the crap out of her once more. How had she not heard him sneak up on her? Sure, he was a shifter, but so was she.

She spun around. "Just a friend."

His lips pressed together, and his breathing was faster than normal. "I heard you talk about the sintor."

Shit. "I was. A friend of a friend recently lost her sintor. I think she said it had run away, and I thought maybe this was her pet."

"Marty found him roaming aimlessly," Stick said.

"Right. Because he ran away. Even if this isn't the same one, she might want to buy another." She hoped that would satisfy him.

"Maybe." He grunted and then stalked off. Okay, that didn't go well.

Chelsea decided Stick might just be the perfect nickname for him because of what he had stuck up his butt. Was that because Toran hadn't run away? In a way, Chelsea hoped this wasn't Marianna's animal. Losing her job over it would really suck.

Not wanting to piss off her employer anymore, she scrubbed out some stalls, and then fed and brushed the cats and dogs. Before she even made it to the larger animals, gravel crunched under tires. An expensive looking car that she couldn't identify rolled to a stop. A tall woman, wearing a white skirt and a sleeveless pink silk shirt, stepped out. Her gaze bounced all over the place.

On the off chance this was Marianna, Chelsea rushed up to her before Stick came out and told her some lie.

"Hi, I'm Chelsea. Can I help you?"

"Chelsea? Oh, thank goodness. I really appreciate you contacting Greer. You said you might have Toran?"

"I'm not sure if he is your pet or not, but come take a look."

As soon as Marianna saw the sintor, she nearly cried, and Toran howled. In fact, her pet made such a racket that Stick came rushing out of the office. "What the devil is going on?"

Chelsea couldn't help but beam. "This is Toran's owner."

"Who's Toran?" He did not sound pleased.

"The sintor."

Without waiting for him to give her permission, Chelsea retrieved the animal from the cage. As soon as he was free, the sintor raced toward Marianna and almost knocked her down. The hugs just kept coming, as did her tears. "Wherever did you find him?" Marianna asked.

Chelsea had to hand it to the woman. From what Chelsea could tell, Marty had stolen the high priced animal.

"One of my workers found him," Stick growled.

"But the fence wasn't broken and the pen was closed."

Damn.

Stick shrugged. "I don't know what to tell you. Do you have any identification to prove this animal belongs to you?"

The woman sniffled and then instructed her pet to settle down. "Yes, I do." She extracted two pieces of paper from her purse and handed them to Stick. "If you look behind Toran's right ear, you'll see a fresh suture mark. He had a cyst removed last week. This is the vet's receipt. The second piece of paper is my receipt from purchasing him three years ago."

Stick glanced at them and then shoved them back at her. "Fine. Next time, make sure your pet doesn't escape."

Please don't say anything, Marianna, Chelsea mentally urged. The last thing she needed was for Stick to believe she'd give him any more trouble. Though if she found out he had asked Marty to steal the expensive animal, the man would wish he'd never opened this place.

After Marianna left, Stick stalked back to his office, not saying anything to her. Fine. Be that way. Chelsea hadn't done anything other than help reunite an owner with her *lost* animal. Too bad she had no idea if Marty had stolen the pet in the hopes of currying favor with Stick or if he'd been instructed to take it.

Once Chelsea finished with her chores, she knocked on the office door. It was past closing time, but she hadn't seen either Stick or Marty for over an hour.

"Come in," Stick said with a less than friendly tone.

"Hey, boss. Is there anything else you'd like me to do before I go?"

"No."

Okay. She could take a hint. Frustrated with how things had gone today, Chelsea left, deciding a nice run in the woods would be just what she could use to blow off some steam.

Fortunately, the trail where Finn had taken her the first day was less than three miles from the shelter. After a short drive, she parked at the trailhead, walked to a large tree, and ditched her clothes. After shifting, she took off at a sprint, needing to release her pent-up frustration. When she arrived at the small waterfall Finn had shown her, she stopped to admire the view. Sticks crunched behind her. When Chelsea spun around, the noise abruptly stopped.

She sniffed the air. Many animals were in the area, but none had a shifter signature. A bird squawked overhead, and she looked up. A crow darted to a tall tree and perched on a limb looking down at her. For a moment, she thought the bird might have been a shifter, but she'd never heard of a crow shifter before.

Her imagination must be getting the best of her. Perhaps it was time to head back. For some reason, the run didn't calm her as much as she'd hoped. A few dark clouds scudded above, casting eerie shadows on the ground. Chelsea wasn't the type to spook, but something was eating at her. Something wasn't right. The question was what?

After she arrived at Finn and Kaleena's condo, she showered and then grabbed a snack, waiting for Kaleena to return home for dinner. Finn wasn't there, because it was one of his evenings to tend bar.

Around six, Kaleena came home. "Hey, how was your day?" she asked.

She told her about Marianna being reunited with her pet. "I heard. Greer called and told me to tell you that Marianna is eternally grateful."

"I'm glad. What I don't understand was why Stick acted so pissed that Marianna was reunited with her lost pet."

"I imagine he was hoping to sell the animal. If the sintor was in good shape, he would have received quite a lot for him."

"Do shelters need any kind of proof of ownership to see the animals?"

Kaleena shook her head. "No."

That didn't seem right. "Out of curiosity, do you know if many people have their pets stolen?"

Kaleena's eyes widened. "I don't know, but I can find out if there has been a sudden increase in missing pets."

"I'd appreciate it." Dread pooled in her stomach at what it might mean for her stay on Tarradon.

Chapter Six

DECLAN LOOKED UP from his desk to find Kaleena looming down at him. "Something wrong?" he asked. "Did I create a public relations nightmare or something?" Declan chuckled, trying to make light of a situation that probably warranted concern.

"No, you're in the clear."

His muscles relaxed. Everyone in his family had stopped in this past week to see if he was okay. The problem was it was hard to hide the dark circles under his eyes, and his dragon refused to heal that woe. "What's the occasion for the visit?"

"It's Chelsea."

At her name, Declan sat up straighter. "What about her?"

Kaleena told him about how Marianna's pet happened to *disappear* from her pen and ended up at the shelter where Chelsea worked.

"Maybe her pet ran away. Sintors are fast little buggers."

"True, but they can't jump over eight foot high fences."

Declan leaned forward. "Do you think the animal had some human—or not so human—help in escaping?"

"Chelsea doesn't know, but she is wondering if the owner is stealing pets in the hopes of reselling them for a large profit. Most of the animals are well-cared for, and well-cared for animals would bring a high price."

Interesting. "If the owner is dirty, and he believes Chelsea knows something, then it would be bad for her. I'll look into it." Boy, would he.

His sister grinned. "I thought you'd say that."

"What's that look for? Is this some ploy to push Chelsea and me together, because if it is, I don't need your help." His dragon was doing a good enough job in trying to get him to ask her out.

She laughed. "I know you can handle yourself, brother dearest. I assure you it's no ploy." She sobered. "I really am worried about her safety though. She is only a wolf shifter."

He pushed back his chair. "I agree, and there's no time like the present to see what's going on."

"Thanks."

With a satisfied look, Kaleena headed back to her office. It was time to see about Chelsea's new employer. Declan stepped into the fresh air. He'd already found the shelter's location, because he'd planned to stop by Chelsea's work to see if the physical attraction still existed. Between the trip to Earth and the rest of the stuff the Guardians were dealing with, it was possible he was merely off his game.

Declan flew to the edge of town and circled a few times to get the lay of the land. The shelter was bordered on three sides by forest. On the south side was a large penned area for the animals to run. He liked that. His aerial view provided him with no evidence of anything unlawful, however.

Once he spotted Chelsea bending over a cage, his dragon shot to life.

What's wrong with you? I know you're horny, but cool it, he yelled at his dragon.

Mate, mate.

Fuck off. Bess was our mate, or did you forget?

His beast didn't answer.

Declan landed. While Chelsea didn't turn around, her back had stiffened, and he didn't know what to think of that. Once in his human form, he walked over to her, shuffling his feet to make noise. The animal she was feeding looked up, and when it growled, Chelsea finally faced him.

Well, I'll be damned. Her eyes were glowing a pretty amber color. Perhaps she pretended not to hear him in order to compose herself.

Kaleena had let it slip that Finn's eyes changed to that color when he was sexually excited—or was that when he was angry?

The problem was that if Chelsea's feelings for him were as strong as what he had been feeling toward her, it was going to make keeping his distance harder.

"Hey, Chelsea." He tried to sound cheerful yet distant. He didn't want to give away the true reason for the visit, and he certainly didn't want to lead her on.

"What are you doing here, Declan? Has something happened to Finn?"

It had never occurred to him that she'd think that. "No." He turned his back to the office to keep his voice from traveling. "Kaleena told me what happened with the sintor," he whispered.

Her eyes widened. "Oh, I see." The office door opened and a tall, thin man exited. "Shit," she whispered. "Pretend you are interested in adopting a pet."

"What do you recommend?" Declan asked loud enough for half the shelter to hear. "My place isn't very large, and I don't have much property for an animal to run around."

She smiled, and his talons nearly pushed through his skin. That was so uncool.

"Many of our animals don't need a lot of space, and I know of quite a few who would love to live with you."

Would you?

Crap. Declan needed to get his head on straight. This was Finn's sister. He didn't need to be making love with Chelsea and then telling her nothing could come of it. Kaleena told him that Chelsea was well aware that he'd already been mated, but from the way she looked at him, she wanted him regardless. Declan had lived long enough to know that she really didn't understand how that kind of relationship never ended well.

"How about a dog?" he asked. "I've always thought I'd enjoy one."

Once more she smiled, and his stupid dragon clawed at his

insides.

"Come around to the side. We have a few you might be interested in."

Once out of sight from the main entrance, Declan could no longer sense the owner's shifter signature. Unless he was mistaken—which was possible with Chelsea next to him—the owner was a lion shifter.

"I have to admit most of these animals are well groomed," he said, putting his mind into investigative mode.

"They are. Do you happen to know if they chip the animals here on Tarradon? I never asked," she said, keeping her voice low.

"Chip them?" he asked.

"That's when a vet inserts a tracking device under the skin. It makes it easier to locate the animal if it becomes lost."

Declan thought the idea rather barbaric, but apparently Chelsea did not. "Not on Tarradon. With so many different types of shifters and unusual species of animals here, those doing the implants might not always be able to tell the difference between humans or true animals. I don't think the shifters would appreciate getting chipped while in their animal form."

"That's too bad. For just regular animals, if they had chips, we could find the rightful owner. To be honest, it isn't that horrible of an idea for shifters either. You never know what different scenarios could happen and having a chip could save a shifter's life."

"That does sound good." Staying at the shelter too long might put her in jeopardy. "How about we discuss your thoughts on the matter over dinner? Say the Highlander's Steakhouse tonight?"

Her eyes glowed, and when she smiled, it appeared as if her teeth had sharpened. Okay, maybe this was a bad idea. Perhaps they could come to some sort of mutual agreement—a very pleasurable one at that—about how to handle this sexual draw.

"I'd love that."

"Are you still staying at my sister's?"

Chelsea nodded. "Yes, but only for a few more days. Kaleena

told me about your dad's cabin near here. He agreed to rent it to me."

"Great. You'll like it. It's real nice." Declan shifted his weight. "How about I pick you up at six?"

"Perfect."

"See you then."

"WHAT DID DECLAN think?" Kaleena asked as soon as Chelsea returned home.

"About what?"

"He said he was going to visit you at the shelter to see if anything strange was going on there."

"You mentioned that to him?" Chelsea was pleased her voice didn't crack.

"Yes. I was worried about you. If some illegal activity is occurring, you don't need to get caught up in a scandal."

"Totally."

Then it had been Kaleena's idea for Declan to stop by and not his. Chelsea had been such a fool to think he'd wanted to see her. She should have figured it out when the first thing he noticed was how well the animals were cared for. Damn.

And to think that as soon as Declan took off, her energy had soared. Most likely it was their potential date—if that was what it was called—that had charged her up.

"Did Declan learn anything?" Kaleena asked again.

"I don't think so. It was hard to talk with Stick sneaking up on us."

"Sneaking up on you?" Kaleena asked.

She waved a hand. "Bad choice of words. He seemed to hover, so Declan and I didn't talk about the possibility of the animals being stolen, which is most likely the reason he asked me out to dinner tonight."

Kaleena beamed. "Ooh. He asked you to dinner? What time is he picking you up?"

"Six."

She glanced at her watch. "Shouldn't you get ready?"

"I am ready. Don't worry, I showered."

Kaleena cocked a brow. "I thought you would want to impress him."

She did. More than anything, but she didn't want to make it obvious that she liked him. "The holes in the jeans are too much? It's all the rage on Earth."

"Where are you going?"

"To The Highlander's Steakhouse."

Kaleena shook her head. "He should have said something so you could have known what to wear. So typical of him. It's fancier than jeans, especially jeans with holes. Try a dress or a skirt. Now scoot, you're losing time."

"Ugh." In truth, Chelsea had already changed three times. Not wanting to embarrass Declan, she decided on a black skirt and a bright Kelly green top that wouldn't make her look washed out. The only way she wouldn't look short next to Declan was if she had one-foot tall heels, which of course, she didn't own.

To prevent Kaleena from suggesting she put on a ton of makeup, Chelsea brushed on some blush and then painted on a slightly darker lipstick shade. After touching up her nearly non-existent eyebrows, she was good to go—or so she hoped.

With her head held high, she stepped into the living room. Whoa. Declan was there—smiling! At her!

His perusal made her face heat up. "Is this okay?" she asked, brushing her palms down her shirt. Her nails began to extend, and her teeth sharpened. Damn.

Stand down, she commanded to her wolf. *Now's not the time.*

Isn't he amazing? her wolf shot back.

Chelsea refused to answer.

"More than okay. Ready?"

"Yes." Chelsea grabbed her purse, happy to have something to do with her hands.

"Have fun, you two," Kaleena said with way too much glee in her voice.

Kaleena acted as if Chelsea had sex planned for after dinner. That was so not true. As much as she wanted to ravish Declan, she had to control her wolf.

Liar.

When Declan held open the door, two of his talons poked through his skin. "Declan?"

He glanced down at his hand and then hid it behind his back. "Sorry. I was thinking about some fires at the edge of the province, and it has me riled up something fierce. I want to find the bastards who are destroying so much land."

Okay, that was a downer. Here she thought he might be excited to be going out with her. Anxiety never made her claws extend—only sexual excitement did.

Chelsea had been hoping the restaurant was far enough away so that he'd fly them there. Being in his arms—or rather his claws—would be wonderful. After they walked east, and passed the parking garage, she figured the restaurant must be close. Oh, well. It was probably for the best.

"I've been doing some research on your situation," Declan began.

"My situation?" She didn't know what he was referring to.

"The fact that Stick might be stealing pets to sell them."

"Oh. What did you find out?" Finally, she could shift her focus from his muscular body and divine scent to something more important.

His hand shot to her waist and stopped her. "Red light."

Crap. Now he'd think she was a space cadet, and usually Chelsea was totally aware of her surroundings. Declan clearly made her come unhinged—mate or no mate.

When the light changed, they crossed the street. "You said you found out something?" Chelsea was finally able to ask with a calm voice.

"Yes, my cousin Anderson Caspian works as a detective at the police department, and I asked him to look into lost or missing pets."

Her heart pulsed. He was her hero. "That was so nice of you."

When Declan looked down at her, her wolf howled, and she had to work hard not to let her nails sharpen once more.

"I hate injustice more than anything, especially when it involves innocent creatures who don't have the means to fully take care of themselves."

She believed in the same thing! Just as Chelsea was about to comment, a blue spark floated in front of her. She blinked, thinking she must have imagined it, until Finn's words came back to her about her being a Wendayan. Her twin had only recently discovered their great grandmother had been a witch.

Either Declan hadn't been looking in that direction or else he decided not to say anything about the random sign. His sister might have let it slip that when Finn was sexually excited, blue sparks flew off his body. She imagined Kaleena's body reacted the same way now that they had mated.

Once they arrived at the restaurant, he escorted her inside. The subdued lighting, soft music, and elegant sconces on the walls made the place quite romantic, but then she reminded herself this wasn't a real date. He was investigating Stick's shelter.

Chelsea decided to wait until they were seated before asking him what his cop cousin had found out. Once at the booth, the waiter handed them menus, but she was too curious right now to think about food. "What did you learn about the missing animals?" she whispered.

"Not a whole lot. Anderson first checked to see whether a business license was registered for the shelter. It was, but he applied only a month ago."

"His sister told me he'd just started. Why would that matter?"

"Ever since *that* date, the number of missing animals has increased substantially."

Her heart squeezed tight. "Is that enough proof for your cousin to investigate? Stick and Marty might be responsible for this increase."

"Anderson will keep an eye out for other anomalies."

Chelsea wasn't sure if she wanted Stick to be guilty, but if he were doing something illegal, he had to be stopped. If he did go to jail, she'd lose her job, but the animals had to be her first concern.

The waiter stopped by with their water. "Anything to drink?"

Declan looked at her. With the day she'd had, she could use something strong. "I'll have a glass of your house red."

"Bring us a bottle," Declan said.

When he looked at her, his eye color softened from that sexy brown to a lighter shade of tan, bordering on green. Was he excited to be with her? Shifter eye color changes were normal on Earth, but what took her by surprise was the quick flash of red under his skin. Finn had told her how he glowed a deep maroon now when he's excited, but she doubted Declan was experiencing lust. Maybe his was his response to the animal injustice.

She refocused on the fact he ordered a whole bottle of wine. Did he plan on getting her drunk and then seducing her? She hoped so though her shifter metabolism was quite good, as must be his.

"I wanted to apologize," Declan said.

"For what?" He'd been wonderful, leaving work to run down her concern about the animals.

"I had to rush out of the party so fast that we never had the chance to chat."

Her pulse raced, and his eyes turned a closer shade to teal. Holy shit. That cast a whole new light on things. "Chat? What about?"

"You."

Be still my beating heart. Her nails extended, forcing her to glance away. Chelsea had to will her eyes not to glow amber, but it was damn hard.

She cleared her throat. "I'm sure my life isn't nearly as exciting as yours. After all, you are a superhero."

His brows rose, along with a cute smile. "How do you figure?"

Declan didn't seem like the type to be fishing for compliments. "You're one of the good guys, if my brother is to be believed."

He leaned back in his seat, his eyes turning brown once more. Before he could ask more about her, the waiter interrupted them with their wine. He placed the bottle on the table and poured each of them a glass. "Have you decided what you'd like to eat?" the man asked.

Too bad Declan wasn't on the menu because the main dish she was thinking of had nothing to do with food.

Chapter Seven

"I 'LL HAVE THE chicken with mushrooms," Chelsea said.

Declan ordered a steak, but he really didn't care what he had, because right now all he could think of was tasting her. His horny, stupid dragon was putting that thought into his head like a rapid-fire automatic weapon. It was bad enough he'd had to hide his hands a few times because his red scales were glowing like a stoplight.

Once he refocused, Declan picked up his drink and held his wineglass with both hands to keep from reaching out and touching her. He loved that she thought of him as a superhero, but it was probably because her brother had exaggerated Declan's exploits. It didn't matter. He certainly wouldn't tell her she was wrong.

"Tell me what your impression is of Tarradon." He was always interested in how others saw this amazing realm. No one asked him about Tarradon when he visited Earth—other than Bess—because he'd never told anyone where he came from.

"I love everything about it. The weather is fantastic, and I especially love how everything is so green and lush. We have waterfalls and hiking trails aplenty in Tennessee, but they are often crowded with people. They tend to freak when they see a wolf, so I'm forced to keep a low profile. We do have one or two areas owned by the shifter community where we can run free however."

He refused to be disappointed that she didn't say having him there made Tarradon perfect. "I can relate. I was frustrated too when I visited Earth because I couldn't shift. We're lucky everyone is aware of shifters on Tarradon."

She smiled, and Declan nearly dropped his glass. Fuck. Her eyes were swirling with flecks of amber, and yes, she had placed her hands on her lap too, implying she was working to control her feelings. His emotions had been frozen inside him for so long, he'd forgotten how to deal with them.

"Let me ask you," Chelsea said. "What do you see as the biggest difference between Earth and Tarradon?"

"You ask hard questions."

Chelsea glanced to the side. "Sorry."

Now you've done it, his dragon said. *Touch her hand and apologize.*

Without thinking, he reached out, and when he pressed his fingers against hers, a bolt of lust raced up his arm and pierced his heart. Declan let go and tried not to look affected, but the glowing red scales couldn't be hidden. Thankfully, Chelsea didn't ask him about them.

"I like hard questions. It makes me think. What is the biggest difference—besides people on Earth not knowing dragons exist?" *Think, think.*

"Yes."

"Probably Earth's view of the universe. Too many think they are alone, when clearly they are not. Most people on Earth don't believe in magic either." He was pleased he'd steered the conversation to safer ground. She nodded, but when she licked her lips, his claws started to extend. As quickly as he could, he thought of the fires the farmers were dealing with, and his talons retracted. Damn, this was hard to be so close to her and not touch her. Chelsea's scent alone was driving him crazy.

"Interesting perspective," she said. "While it is true that we on Earth are in denial about a lot of things, it makes us who we are: hopeful though shortsighted. We're also dreamers. When you don't know what's out there, you can make up anything you want!"

He laughed. "I like you, Chelsea McKinnon."

She blushed, and her eyes turned a full-blown amber color, which turned him on even more. "I like you too," she said.

Damn, he shouldn't have said that, but he had meant it. Thankfully, the food arrived, which gave him something to focus on instead of her. He dug in, trying to think of what else to ask her that would sound like something his father might want to know. His dad was good at making people feel comfortable.

"Have you decided how long you're going to stay? Or does it depend on what happens with the shelter?" he asked, hoping it was a safe topic.

She stuffed a piece of chicken in her mouth, chewed, and then washed it down with some wine, possibly to stall. "I'm not sure. I suppose if Finn and Kaleena go back to Earth at some point, I'll go with them if only to check out my employment opportunities there. That's assuming Stick's shelter folds."

He tried to understand her motivation. "Staying here depends on money then?"

Her brows furrowed. Damn him and his big mouth. He hadn't meant it to sound like a criticism. If he were honest though, part of him had been hoping her real reason for staying had something to do with wanting to be around him.

No! No! What was he thinking? He didn't want that. It would only make things harder if she threw herself at him.

"Money is my biggest concern. I can't rely on Finn and Kaleena to take care of me. If this job goes south, I'll have to come up with something."

"I'm sure there are a lot of opportunities here on Tarradon for you." *Especially if a Sinclair put in a good word for you.* From what he knew of Chelsea though, if she found out her employment was based on a favor, she'd be pissed. Damn. Declan decided he'd be better off keeping his mouth shut. Besides, if Chelsea returned to Earth, he wouldn't be tormented any longer.

The rest of the dinner involved them finishing their food. There were so many things he wanted to ask her about—like her beliefs on injustice and her thoughts on fighting to name a few—but he didn't want to make her skittish or excite his dragon even more if her passionate response resonated with his beliefs.

His back-and-forth attitude was driving him crazy. He needed to decide if he wanted her to stay or leave. Chelsea looked up at him and smiled. Damn it. She might not be his mate, but nothing prevented him from hooking up with her, as long as they both understood what they were getting themselves into.

Bottom line, Chelsea deserved a mate. He did worry that in the throes of passion, he might bite her. It was possible that would hurt her a lot since she wasn't his mate. It wasn't like she'd change into a dragon if he did.

"Declan?" she asked.

When he returned his focus to her, she nodded to their server who was holding the check. Damn. He grabbed the bill. "Hold on a sec."

He lifted his phone from his pocket, clicked on the app to add a generous tip, and then pressed it against the machine in the man's hand to transfer the money between his account and the restaurant's.

"Thank you, sir. Ma'am. Have a nice evening."

Declan turned to Chelsea. "Ready?"

"Yes."

Declan helped Chelsea out of the booth, but touching her reignited his simmering passion. As they headed to the exit, his mind spun. All evening, his lust had been building, and if he didn't do something about it soon, his dragon might revolt. Declan certainly didn't need to have his claws fully extend, his scales glow, or his teeth sharpen when he walked her to her door.

He had no doubt she was just as interested in a little fling as he was, but she was Finn's twin sister. If Declan broke her heart, Kaleena and Finn would never forgive him.

As they walked to his sister's condo, his noble nature crumbled. He and Chelsea were both consenting adults. What harm could come of a sexual relationship as long as both parties understood that it was an itch-scratching thing and not a permanent situation?

I want her forever, his dragon moaned.

We were given our one chance.

Once Declan figured out that he might be able to rid Chelsea from his mind and heart if they spent some time between the sheets, his thinking cleared. This quick hot affair could not take place at his sister's condo though, and he wasn't going to wait until she moved into the family's cabin. He needed her tonight.

"It's kind of early. How would you like to go someplace where you can see all of the city lights?"

The intake of breath told him all he needed to know. Chelsea didn't want this date to end either.

"Are we driving or *flying?*" She sounded excited when she said the last word.

He had intended to drive, but if they flew, he could take her to a more secluded spot. "Flying works for me. We'll head back to my sister's condo and take off from there."

She clapped and his insides melted. Chelsea's innocence and enthusiasm really spoke to him. "Is your truck parked there?"

"Yes."

"Can I leave my purse inside? I don't want to drop it when we fly. I'd leave it at the condo, but I'd rather not get the second degree from your sister."

"I totally agree. Don't worry. It will be safe since I'll lock it up in back."

Once at Kaleena's condo, she stashed her purse. They then took the elevator to the top floor, where they climbed to the rooftop. "Face up or face down," he asked.

She chuckled. "Face down, please. I want to see everything."

He loved her adventurous spirit. "Okay then."

Declan stepped back and shifted.

"Wow," she said as she reached out a hand and touched his wing, her finger lingering over one of his red scales interspersed with the black. "You're beautiful."

If he'd been able to speak, he'd have told her men weren't sup-posed to be beautiful. A better description might have been powerful or magnificent.

With care, he lifted her in his claw and tucked her against his chest. The moment her body was snuggled against him, his dragon shot out a five-foot stream of fire. *Watch it, fire breath*, he chastised.

Chelsea looked over her shoulder. "That was awesome."

At least she hadn't freaked. He just didn't want her to think he was showing off—his dragon had been.

Declan flapped his wings and soared upward. The night sky, fresh air, and the fact he had Chelsea in his arms—or rather his claws—bolstered his spirits. The longer they flew, the more excited he became over the potential outcome of tonight's adventure. He debated flying her to his dad's cabin and enjoying some wine, surrounded by the forest. While he had a spare key, he decided he wanted something more romantic.

I like romance, his dragon said with glee.

I just want Chelsea to have a good time. Nothing more.

His inner animal didn't seem to understand, but Declan didn't want to outline his real plan for fear his animal would go crazy.

Hmm. Where was the most romantic spot in Tarradon? There were caves in the middle of the realm where the provinces met, but at night they'd be too dark, even for their shifter sight, not to mention uncomfortably damp.

Wait a minute. He had just the place. Declan changed direction and headed to the hills where the top of the mountain was covered in yellow meadow flowers this time of year. Without the light pollution of the city, the stars would be amazing too. Where he had in mind, a small spring bubbled out of the side of a rock face that cascaded down the mountainside. While they would be too high to see where the falls pooled, they'd be able to hear it.

Ten minutes later, he set her down on the mountain crest and then shifted back. Chelsea opened her arms and spun around. "This is incredible."

"I agree." He moved closer. "Just listen," he whispered, as he stood behind her with his hands on her shoulders.

She didn't move, no doubt her shifter hearing peaking. "I hear water."

"Yes." He stepped to her side and held out his hand. "I'll show you where."

Feeling like he was twenty years old again, he held her hand as they traipsed over the field toward the pure water source. Once at the rock face, Declan dropped down on one knee. "Take a drink," Declan said.

Chelsea knelt beside him and scooped up the water. They each drank their fill.

"I've never tasted anything so pure," she said.

Her enthusiasm was infectious. "Not only is the water the purest up here, we can see the stars as well."

Declan stretched out on his back, supporting his head with his hands, and crossed his feet at the ankles. The ground was softly tufted with grass and flowers, so he didn't feel guilty when Chelsea lay next to him. He refused to think how easy it would be to roll over, gather her in his arms, and make love to her. For the moment, he was content to show her his world.

"I've never seen anything like this before." Awe filled her voice.

He chuckled. "I hope not. I realize Tarradon is a parallel universe, but our star alignment is different from yours."

"No Orion's Belt? Or North Star?"

"Actually, we can see them at certain times of the year. Look over here." Declan lifted his arm. "There's the North Star."

"Oh, I see it now. We're not so different after all."

"No. Not so different at all." People wanted to connect with others no matter where they were in the universe.

She rolled onto her side and propped up her head, balancing on her elbow. "The view here is breathtaking."

He looked over at her. Chelsea wasn't looking at any celestial bodies. Hmm. "If I flew you farther from the city, it would be even more spectacular."

Declan twisted toward her, their lips inches from each other. It took all of his control not to kiss her, though from the way she was looking at him, it was what she wanted him to do.

Could he just kiss her and then stop?

Do it! Do it! his dragon urged.

"What I'm seeing right now is spectacular enough," she said as blue sparks shot off her arms.

"Chelsea?"

"Yes?"

He tried to catch another blue spark that darted off her, but it turned out to be light. Declan chuckled. "Are you trying to tell me something?" If it had been brighter, he bet he would have seen her blush.

She lifted one shoulder. "That blue stuff? It's new to me too, but it just means I find you...interesting, that's all."

He laughed. "Just *interesting*?"

Chelsea reached out and ran her hand down his arm. "Perhaps a little bit more. What about you? You're glowing. Am I interesting too?"

"You are."

She leaned in closer, and her scent ramped up his desires past the point where he could stop.

"What are we going to do about it?" she asked, her voice breathy.

Declan cupped her face, and a blast of heat and lust electrified him. His chest began to scale over, and his talons poked out the end of his fingers. *Stop it!*

He tossed her a fake frown. "I'm not sure."

"Really? Is there anything I can do to help you figure it out?"

"Maybe." Before she asked what that was, Declan leaned over and kissed her.

Big, big, big mistake. Or was it? Not only did his body make the grass glow red, his talons fully poked out of his fingertips, forcing him to release her face. His teeth had sharpened but so had hers. Damn, it was hard to kiss someone who turned him on like this. Desperate to calm down, he forced the image of Bess into his head, but the picture refused to form. It was almost as if she had been a figment of his imagination.

Chelsea groaned, and then pressed on his shoulder to roll him onto his back once more. Declan couldn't have stopped her even if he'd wanted to. A second later, she crawled on top of him, drew in her knees, and straddled him. His mind blanked.

She leaned back and supported herself with her hands on his thighs. Looking up at the sky, she sighed. "This is just an amazing view."

"It's about to get a whole lot better now too." Declan couldn't take her teasing ways any longer and slipped his hands under her shirt. When she didn't flinch or try to stop him, he continued until he'd palmed her breasts—breasts that were small yet deliciously firm. "Wouldn't you be more comfortable without all these clothes on?"

That sounded cheesy even to him, but Declan hadn't tried to pick up a woman since his mate had died. An ache of guilt shot through him, until her dying words came back to him. Bess had unconditionally loved him, but she'd made him promise to find happiness if she wasn't around any longer.

Bess would be happy for him.

Chelsea sat up, returning him to the present. "Will you help me?"

He grinned. "Don't mind if I do." She leaned forward, and Declan obliged by lifting the shirt over her head. The sliver of moonlight illuminated her pink bra—or else it was his glowing scales that were providing the light.

He ran a thumb over both nipples, which he could feel had started to harden, jumpstarting his libido something fierce. How could a union that wasn't sanctioned by the Fates feel so right?

In a less than a smooth move, he pinched the back of her bra to unhook it. Being out of practice, it wasn't until the third attempt that it popped open. As seductively as he could, he lowered the straps, exposing the most perfect breasts he'd ever seen. "You are so beautiful."

"So are you."

This shouldn't be about him but rather about what kind of connection they could achieve. Letting his dragon rule for once, he pulled her close and kissed her hard. When she ran her tongue along the seam of his lips, Declan's body pulsed with intense desire. Thankfully, his claws remained retracted. Both he and his dragon wanted to touch her more, so he slid his hands down her naked back and clasped her waist. The urge to mount her was strong, but he wanted Chelsea to dictate the speed. The last thing he wanted was to mislead her.

She continued to taste him as she lifted his shirt from his jeans. The second her hands touched his chest though, the scales on his back hardened. *Not now, you idiot*, he said, chastising his dragon.

Sorry.

A second later, Declan was all human—that is except for his glowing scales under his skin. Chelsea sat up and lifted his shirt. "Where is there light when a girl needs some?"

Declan laughed and lifted his arm, providing her with more illumination. "Does this help?"

"I think you need to take off the shirt so I can get a better view." She leaned back to allow him to sit up enough to remove it. Once he did, he tossed it next to him.

"That's better," she said.

"Better would be if you were totally naked." He reached up and tapped her nose.

"Ooh. That's easy enough." She slid off him and rolled onto her back. After kicking off her shoes, Chelsea lifted up her skirt and slipped off her panties.

Declan's dragon roared. Before she had the chance to climb back on, he was on his knees. "Let me taste you first."

He didn't even wait for her to answer before he was on his stomach between her thighs. One hand twirled her distended nipple between his fingertips while he opened her folds with his other. He inhaled deeply, her scent making him dizzy with desire. No surprise, the first lick nearly electrified him. Never had he experienced anything as exciting—or as forbidden. Not wanting this moment to end, he fondled the other breast while he licked and flicked her tiny pearl.

"Oh, Declan. Yes!"

Chelsea clamped a hand on his head and held on tight. With her feet planted on the ground, she lifted her hips, and her short skirt lightly brushed his face.

Needing to take her higher, when he slipped two fingers into her opening, blue sparks shot off every part of her body. Her nails, which were digging into the back of his head, had sharpened to the point of being painful.

When she opened her mouth and gulped in air, her inner walls tensed. Chelsea moaned and groaned, wiggling right and left. She sucked in a large breath, and then a loud yell burst from her lips as her climax claimed her.

Like a popped balloon, her hands dropped to the ground and her body sagged. "Oh, my goddess, Declan. That was pure heaven."

He chuckled. "I hope you aren't finished. I've only just begun."

She lifted her head and smiled. "Not by a long shot."

Chapter Eight

C HELSEA HAD NEVER experienced anything so sensational in her life. All Declan had done was press two fingers on her sweet spot as he licked her, and she'd gone off like a rocket. Fate might not think he was her mate, but he or she was dead wrong. It didn't matter to her what the gods proclaimed. Her body told her they were meant to be together.

Whatever Declan was willing to give her, she'd take and enjoy.

With a huge effort, she pushed up on her elbows. "Let me return the favor."

Declan chuckled. "Wolf lady, there is no way I would last if your mouth was on my dick. I do not want to embarrass myself."

"Chicken."

"We'll see who's chicken when I impale you."

"Hard to do with your pants on."

"I can change that," he said.

Faster than she could count to three, he was naked and sporting a raging hard on that made her wonder if he would even fit inside her. "Dragons definitely are bigger than wolf shifters—or any other kind of shifters for that matter." Chelsea reached out to touch his big cock.

Declan let her grab it. "Think of it as a stick of dynamite."

Chelsea couldn't help but crack up. "How about showing me some of your explosive power then?"

Declan focused on her face as he crawled on top of her. "I want you bad, Chelsea McKinnon."

She cupped his face. "Then have me."

What happened next defied description. Her body turned into an inferno, shooting off an array of blue sparks, while Declan's body pulsed red. They looked like a mini light show.

She expected him to plunge right in, but instead, he lowered his head and sucked on one nipple and then the other. Holy sparks that felt good. It could be that brilliant stars were overhead, the night air was balmy, or the fact that the man of her dreams was lavishing amazing attention on her, but Chelsea had never been happier.

"Is it safe?" he asked in between sucking her tits.

She assumed he meant if she could get pregnant. Right after Declan had returned to Tarradon, Chelsea had taken the hormone shot to prevent pregnancy. "Yes."

"Good, because I didn't bring any condoms."

When he dragged his slightly sharpened teeth across one nipple and tugged, waves of erotic lust shot straight to her pussy. If he didn't take her now, she might combust on him—or worse, shift.

"Before my wolf makes an unwanted appearance, I suggest you show me what you got."

Declan lifted his head and kissed her. "Ready to put the stars to shame?"

She wasn't quite sure what he meant, but it sounded good. "More than ready."

He widened her legs with his knees and slid his huge cock straight into her. Holy shifting constellations. His dick was wider than wide.

She inhaled, trying to absorb the intensity and stretching. When Declan reached the end, he stilled, as if he too needed a moment to compose himself. As the slight pain ebbed, Chelsea's desires grew once more.

Declan might not technically be her mate, but there was no reason not to pretend that he was, even if it were only for a short time.

"Need you," Declan whispered.

Those two words melted her heart, and the kiss that followed made her believe in a happily ever after. *Fuck you, Fate. This is where I need to be.*

Declan eased out and then slowly slid in again. With each stroke, her passion grew. She touched his face, his shoulders, his back, and oh, yes, his hard buns of steel. Everything about Declan was perfect.

"I can't get enough of you," he said.

"I'm open to you trying as hard as you need to." Chelsea was never this bold, but Declan brought out the sass in her.

As if he'd been waiting for permission, he drove in once more, withdrew, and then plowed in again. Not one to be a bystander, she thrust her hips upward and met him stroke for stroke. Her blue light skidded over Declan's skin, kissing the red scales lit from within. The magic amped up her need and desire so high, her breath lodged in her throat. The blue sparks practically proved he was her mate. Right?

"Chel-sea!"

Declan's desperate plea ignited every inch of her body and sent her spiraling over the climactic cliff. Her orgasm claimed her so hard, she forgot to breathe. A second later, Declan's cock exploded.

Neither moved. A minute passed.

And then another.

He finally dropped his head to her shoulder and rolled them over so that she was sprawled out on top of him. He patted her back. "The stars have never been brighter."

She wasn't sure if he was talking about the real stars or what they just experienced. "The light show was something else."

"Amen."

She didn't know how long they remained in each other's arms, since they both might have fallen asleep.

Declan kissed the top of her head. "I think we should head back. I don't want your brother looking for us and beating the shit out of me."

Slowly, she crawled off him. "He wouldn't dare. I'm happy, and that's all that matters to Finn."

"I hope you're right." He patted her butt. "We need to clean up."

While the water from the spring was cold, it did the trick. After they dressed, the trip back to the condo was bittersweet. Now more than ever, she needed to move out of Kaleena and Finn's condo so she might be able to convince Declan to spend the night.

THE NEXT DAY at work, Chelsea was in such a good mood. The sun seemed brighter and the animals calmer. Most likely, her wards were keying off her emotions.

She'd already cleaned the cages and fed the animals before Marty arrived. He'd brought four more animals to the shelter. At some point, they would have to find someplace else to take them—or else build more cages.

She'd only seen two customers show up to buy animals since she'd started working there, making her wonder how Stick managed to stay afloat. He was the one who took care of the transactions, so she had no idea how much anyone paid, but she doubted it was enough to sustain the upkeep. For all she knew, the province subsidized the place. Rules on Tarradon might be completely different than on Earth.

"Can you help me, Chelsea?" Marty called out. He opened the back of his truck and lifted a cardboard box.

She rushed over to him. "What do you have there?" She looked inside. "It's a litter of kittens. How adorable."

"Yeah, the mom couldn't take care of them."

She took the box from him. "Don't you worry, little ones, I'll take good care of you."

"I also have two dogs in the back, but I'll take them in."

She wondered if they were injured, but she'd find out soon enough. Once inside the office, she checked over the kittens. They were mewing up a storm, all seemingly in need of some milk and some loving. Chelsea could provide both.

She spent the entire morning making sure her new wards were happy and free of any apparent injury. Stick had taken the two dogs into the back to treat them. Marty told her Stick was a vet, which kind of surprised her seeing how the man didn't exude much emotion. She might be biased because the vet back in Silver Lake was so conscientious and caring.

"How about putting the kittens outside in cage number seven?" Stick said as he walked out from the back room. "It has a heated floor."

"I didn't realize you had that. Cool." She might have misjudged the man.

Stick tossed her a brief smile. Happy the kittens would be safe, Chelsea went about her business, caring for the other animals. She'd just finished getting them settled when an expensive looking car drove in and parked. Out popped Sabrina, Stick's sister.

The woman smiled and came over to her. "How's the new job going?" she asked.

"Great. Thanks for telling me about it."

"My brother says you're doing a good job."

Heat flushed her face. "I try."

"How are you settling in?"

Stick must have told her she was from Earth. "I've met a few people." And one amazing man.

"If you ever want to blow off some steam, let me know." Sabrina smiled and then walked toward the office, probably to help out.

While the woman seemed friendly enough, Chelsea found the conversation a bit odd, maybe because Sabrina and she seemed so different. While Chelsea wasn't adverse to nice clothes and even wore some makeup on occasion, she wondered how Sabrina could afford the nice car and fancy clothes on a receptionist's salary.

Whatever. Chelsea didn't need to be thinking about Sabrina. She had a job to do.

DECLAN HADN'T BEEN able to concentrate all day. His mood swings were driving him—and no doubt anyone else he came in contact with—crazy. Making love with Chelsea had been off the charts good, but he needed to be careful. The last thing he wanted was to hurt her feelings. While he wanted to spend every minute with her, it would be wise to keep his distance today before asking her out again. Kaleena had said that Chelsea would be moving into their father's cabin tomorrow, which would afford him a good excuse to see her then.

No matter how much he rationalized why he needed to stay away, his dragon refused to accept it. Flying over her workplace would give him a chance to see her and to make sure she was okay. He could always cloak himself if she was working outside.

When Declan popped his head into his brother's office, Stone was hunched over the desk. "Just a heads up. I'm leaving for a bit. I need to check something out, but I won't be gone long," Declan said.

Stone straightened. "Everything okay?"

No. I'm fighting with my dragon. I need to stay away from Chelsea, but I can't seem to function without her. "Just have to do a little surveillance."

"Good luck." Stone went back to studying what was on his screen. His youngest brother ran the business end of the Sinclair mines, whereas Logan oversaw the Caspian mine business, and Declan couldn't be any prouder of them.

Once outside, he shifted and headed for the animal shelter. He hadn't noticed anything illegal when he'd circled before, but with more time, he might spot something. Chelsea had said that Marty was the one to find the animals. Following him might be the best use of his time, but given it was late in the day, he'd have to conduct that tail at another date.

Making certain that Chelsea was okay needed to be his first

concern.

When he drew near the forested area, Declan cloaked himself. If Chelsea saw him, she'd wonder why he hadn't called, especially since last night had been world-altering for him—and probably for her too.

As he came closer, he spotted a black Lambright in the drive, and his heart jumped. His former girlfriend, Sabrina Parnell, drove a car like that. Oh, shit. Her brother Seth had been in vet school at the time they dated, which was why Declan had never met him. Seth could be Stick.

Some tall woman was talking with Chelsea—a woman who looked very much like Sabrina from the back. Declan dove closer, careful not to let the air from his wing flaps give away his presence. When he moved in front of the mystery woman, his claws tightened. It was her. He could only hope Sabrina was merely making small talk with her brother's employee. There was no way Sabrina knew that Chelsea and he had hooked up.

Stick would know Chelsea's last name, but because Finn was new to the realm, he doubted the vet would connect Finn with Declan.

Needing a moment to clear his head, Declan soared upward. Hoping this was an innocent encounter, he did a few more circles, looking for anything illegal. Once Sabrina headed inside and Chelsea went back to work, Declan took off, more unsettled than ever.

Chapter Nine

YESTERDAY HAD BEEN stressful. Chelsea had waited for Declan to call and confess his undying lust for her, but he hadn't. She tried to remind herself that Declan managed the Sinclair and Caspian mines, and that his job was important. Not only that, they weren't mates. Chelsea had gone into this affair merely for sex, knowing that it could be nothing more, but now she had to admit she'd been lying to herself. Damn. The slow wave of depression that had washed over her had to be a result of her wanting all of him. Too bad that could never be.

Thank goodness, she loved her job. The licks and joy she received from the animals helped get her through the day. She had the next two days off, and she planned to spend the time moving into Kaleena's father's cabin. Kaleena had driven her by the place three days ago, and Chelsea had fallen in love with the cute, cozy, wood home that reminded her of something she often saw in Silver Lake.

The best part of the Sinclair cabin? She could walk out of the front door and go for a run. It couldn't be more perfect. Yes, it was isolated, but she'd be safe. Being a shifter had a lot of advantages.

Just as she was about to clock out for the day, Marty waltzed in and waved to her. "Got a few more rescues," he called out, sounding more cheerful than usual. "I need your help."

Curious what new animals he had, she followed him. In the back of his truck sat three crates. One contained a large black dog that appeared to be asleep. She didn't recognize the breed, but the animal looked healthy. The other two seemed to belong to the cat family—leopard perhaps? They were truly beautiful. Given they weren't moving, they probably had been sedated. "Are they okay?" she asked.

"They will be soon once the tranquilizer wears off."

"I'll get the cart," she said. Chelsea jogged to the side of the building and dragged the wheeled structure back over.

Once she lined it up to the back of Marty's tailgate, the two of them lugged the crates onto it. "Help me take them to the side bay. I can handle it from there."

While Marty pushed the cart, Chelsea guided it. "Where did you find these beautiful animals?" she asked.

"One of the cats was trapped in some barbed wire fence. Once I freed him, his mate came out. I hated to separate them so I took them both."

She looked at each of the black animals but couldn't detect any injuries. "Why did you sedate them? Why not let them go free?"

"Stick always likes to make sure they are healthy first before we release them into the wild."

She let out a breath. "That's awesome. And the dog? What kind is he?"

"We call him a Labdron. I've been to Earth a few times. They are like your Labrador Retrievers."

"Ah." They reached the entrance. "You sure you don't need help?"

"Nope. I'll get Stick to give me a hand. He'll need to check them over."

Marty acted as if Stick were the hired help, instead of the other way around. "Okay then. I'll see you in a couple of days."

"Enjoy your weekend." He rushed inside.

As much as she wanted to stay with the animals to make sure they'd be fine, she sensed Marty wouldn't like it. Quite a few people she'd met on Tarradon seemed different than those on Earth. Marty and Stick were two of them.

As Chelsea drove back to the condo, she decided that many of the Tarradonians needed some lessons in keeping to their side of the road. This reinforced her desire to live in the country. Where she'd go for food when she was far from the town center, she didn't know, but she'd figure it out.

Thank goodness, Kaleena had added her to the eye scanner. Chelsea let herself into the condo. "Hello?"

No one was there. Darn. Finn might have left for the bar already, and apparently Kaleena was still at work. Chelsea didn't want to think about either one having to battle with someone and put their lives in jeopardy. She shivered at that terrible thought.

Because it was still light out, she decided to check out the cabin, if only to make a list of what things she'd need. Kaleena had texted her during lunch to say her dad had dropped off the key. It would be on the counter if Chelsea wanted to see the interior.

Excited, she grabbed the keychain and headed back out. Due to rush hour, the trip took about thirty minutes instead of twenty. She thought she would have remembered where the cabin was located, but once she turned off onto a dirt road, she became confused. The road forked twice, and because the sun was setting, she didn't want to get lost.

Deciding it would be best to let her wolf do the tracking, she parked by the side of the road and headed into the forested area. On Earth, she wasn't self-conscious about undressing when in front of other shifters, but she didn't know if non-dragon shifters from Tarradon remained clothed after a shift or not.

She hadn't passed anyone in the last five minutes, so changing shouldn't be an issue—nor would leaving her clothes at the base of a tree. Slipping behind a large elm, she undressed and set her folded clothes on an elevated root.

Once she shifted, she took off, inhaling the fresh scent of the forest. After a quick and invigorating run, she spotted the cabin. Yes! She had been on the right road.

Oh, my. Declan was there. What was up with that?

What to do? What to do? It wasn't as if she could shift back and walk inside naked though. Chelsea wasn't the type to flaunt herself like that. The only choice was to race back to the tree for her clothes, hike to the car, and drive back in—which was what she did.

As she pulled next to Declan's truck, he stepped onto the porch and smiled. Her heart actually fluttered, as images of coming home to him every day like this surfaced.

Stop with the fantasy. It would only make it worse when it ended.

Regardless of what she told herself, she couldn't help but lust over his appearance with his button down black shirt, jeans, and boots.

Trying to appear unaffected by his presence, she slid out of the car. "Hey. What are you doing here?" she asked as he stood on the porch steps.

"I wanted to make sure it was clean inside for when you moved in."

"That is so sweet of you. I've yet to look inside. When Kaleena drove me by, she didn't have a key, so I never had the chance to see it."

He smiled and her insides twisted. "Then come on in."

When she stepped past him, the urge to kiss him nearly made her miss a step, possibly because his upper chest was actually glowing red. It went without saying that she was shooting off blue sparks like there was no tomorrow. What was up with that? Declan wasn't her mate. Or had she been misinformed about when her blue sparks would appear? Perhaps being on Tarradon triggered the change.

"How about a hello kiss?" Declan said with a cheeky grin—an expression she'd rarely seen before.

Chelsea's bones melted. "One kiss. That's it. If we start, we might not stop."

He laughed. "You are right, but what's wrong with that?" When he held up a hand, she tilted her head. "Look, I get it. We should probably talk about what is happening between us. I mean we can never be mates, but do you still want to…"

Screw? Hell, yes. "What do *you* want to do?" She dragged a finger down his chest, her body almost exploding from being so close to him.

"Whatever you want."

That was a cop-out answer. "Can it hurt to enjoy each other until we grow tired of being with each other?"

He cupped her face. "You are an amazing woman, Chelsea. I wish I could give you more, but we both know we aren't mates, so until your Fated mate comes along…"

"We can enjoy each other?"

"I'm game if you are."

Her breath lodged in her throat. No amount of rational thought could make her say no. "Yes."

He closed the door behind her and pressed her up against it. A part of her wanted to look around the adorable cabin first—but only a very tiny part. The rest of her wanted to devour him.

When he leaned in and kissed her, fire consumed her. Her wolf howled, sharpening her teeth and her nails. When Chelsea ran her hands up his back, it was like rubbing her fingers over metal. Was he trying not to shift too? The sudden image of scales covering his body shook her.

She broke the kiss. "Declan?"

His half closed eyes eased open. "Yes?"

"What's happening to your back?"

He stiffened. "You happened."

"I don't understand."

He stepped back and motioned she enter the living room. "When I'm excited, my dragon likes to make his presence known. You know how my scales glow?"

"Yes, and I become a light show apparently."

"Both of our eyes change color and our teeth sharpen, but dragons do other things. I've heard some kind of shifters grow hair, but we grow scales."

Now she was intrigued. She stepped toward him. "How about taking off your shirt and show me?"

He laughed, lifted the material over his head, and ditched it. "The scales have disappeared now, but if you want to kiss me again, I imagine my dragon can accommodate you."

"I like the kissing part."

He held up his hands. "Because I love your sparks, how about taking off your top so I can see more of them?"

She punched him in the chest. "Ow. Is sex all you think about?" It was all she thought about.

He moved closer, his eyes flashing teal. "No, but when you're near, I can't help myself."

Chelsea totally got that they would never be mates, but life was short, and she wanted to enjoy him.

Declan loomed over her and lifted off her shirt slowly, as if he was waiting for her to tell him to stop. To show him what she wanted, she grabbed his crotch.

He grinned, his teeth rather pointed. "You aren't playing fair."

"Like you are?" she asked.

"Good point." He tossed off her top and let it fall to the wooden floor.

Declan stepped back, ditched the boots, and then his jeans and briefs. He towered over her in all his glory. Wow.

Not able to wait, Chelsea reached out and grabbed his naked dick, which was larger than she remembered.

Declan sucked in a breath. "Be careful."

"I was careful last night. Now? No way." Without waiting for him to respond, she knelt in front of him and drew him deep into her mouth.

As she pumped her fist up and down, his hissed. She kind of wanted him to come—for her ego of course—but she also wanted to feel his heat inside her. When the first signs of his salty tang tinged her tongue, he clasped her shoulders and drew her to her feet.

"No more. I'm way too close and desperately want to be inside of you."

She smiled. A second later, their hands were all over each other, as were their lips. Chelsea pressed her hips against his naked body. Wanting more contact, she stepped back. "I need to take my clothes off."

"I was thinking the same thing," he said.

Together they fumbled with her shorts while she kicked off her sandals. With a quick pinch, her bra was history. Now naked, Chelsea returned to ravishing Declan, the man she was learning was hard to stay away from.

"I love the way you taste," he mumbled after their long tongue twisting experience.

"Mmm." One hand found her breast while his palm pressed between her legs. She moaned, embarrassed by her weakness around him. "Take me now," she panted.

Declan lifted her up by the waist and walked her backward until she was pressed against the door. He then lifted her arms above her head and kissed her hard again.

She melted. His scent, touch, and taste incited every nerve ending in her body. Desperate for his cock, she slipped out of his hold and threaded her arms around his neck as she wrapped her legs around his waist. "I need you bad," she whispered.

Declan lowered his lips to her neck and slipped his dick straight into her opening. The second he let go, she dropped down on him. Fireworks exploded—or were those bursts of light all coming from her? It didn't matter; Chelsea wanted it all.

For a split second, she thought he might bite her only to remember it didn't matter if he did—they could never mate. She must have stiffened because Declan dragged his lips across her chin and then up to her mouth. Need pummeled her.

Declan slipped out of her only long enough to drive right back in. Something inside of her snapped, and she joined in the fray, lifting and dropping. As they kissed, he kept hammering into her, bringing her closer and closer to a massive climax. She rubbed her palms over his head and then down his face, loving the rough bristles, unable to get enough of him.

Their tongues darted in and out, tasting and competing for space. When he pressed her harder against the door and slipped his hands to her waist, she lost it. On the next thrust, her climax erupted, and Declan detonated a second later, his teal eyes glassing over. It was almost as if he left this realm for a moment.

Chelsea broke the kiss to suck in air. Burying his face between her shoulder and cheek, he wrapped his arms around her and held on tight. Even though she understood that Tarradon hadn't tilted on its axis, it sure felt like something monumental had happened.

A minute later, he walked them through the living room to the kitchen and set her down on the tile countertop. He then uncoupled. "I'll find something to clean us up with."

Declan's gaze remained a bit unfocused. Thankfully, neither one voiced what they probably were both thinking: what the hell had just happened? Sure, they were attracted to each other, but it was as if their animals had pushed them aside and attacked each other.

Declan wet a cloth and brought it over. She cleaned up, and then handed him the clean end to finish the job on himself.

Once he tossed the towel in the sink, he opened the refrigerator. He looked back over his shoulder. "Water, soda, or beer?"

She had no idea what their sodas tasted like, and water wouldn't give this adventure its proper due. "A beer would be great."

Chapter Ten

A S THEY DRESSED, Declan chastised himself. Yes, he'd told her their relationship was all about sex, but to basically attack her the second she walked in the door was just plain wrong. He'd never done anything like that before.

"Let's sit for a moment and have our drinks before I give you a brief tour," he said.

After Chelsea slipped on her clothes and Declan pulled on pants, they sat down on the sofa beside each other. Their attraction was out of hand, and it was up to him to set things straight.

Where should he begin? "I feel as if I should apologize for practically jumping you as soon as you got here. Believe me, I'm not in the habit of ravishing a woman before she has a chance to barely get through the door."

When Chelsea looked off to the side, his gut churned. She twisted toward him. "In case you didn't notice, I participated equally in the encounter. Besides, we agreed to keep this strictly sexual. You were hot for me. I was hot for you. There's nothing wrong with that."

No, there wasn't, only he didn't believe her. "That's true, but as much as I want this to be strictly sexual, it feels more than that." He lifted Chelsea's hand to his lips. "Hell, when I first met you, I actually thought I'd been given a second chance at having a mate. How crazy is that?"

"It's not crazy, but I've never heard of anyone having two mates."

"And therein lies the problem. Chelsea, clearly I want you. I can't stop thinking about you, in fact, so much so that my work is suffering."

"Whoa." The light in her eyes extinguished.

"I know, right?" She wasn't making it any easier on him. "I think we should limit our contact from now on."

Her brows pinched. "Because?"

"Like I said—if I know I can see you any time of day or night, I'll be preoccupied, and I have bad guys to catch and a company to run."

"Why not give it a few more days? Maybe we'll be tired of each other by then."

He huffed out a laugh. "I don't think that is going to happen. I don't understand any of this. The sex is off the charts. That should be enough, but for some reason, it's not. Besides, it's not fair to you if we pretend we're this happy couple."

She sat up straighter. "Why not?" Chelsea lifted the beer to her lips and took a long hit. He hoped it wasn't for fortification.

"Because the longer we are together, the harder it will be to separate when you do find your mate—and you will find him. I don't know if he's here or on Earth, but when you say goodbye to me, I'll be devastated again." He was babbling, but he couldn't help it. "I don't want to sound pathetic, but I've been through that kind of pain before, and I don't want to repeat it."

The bottle she was twirling in her hands looked like a lifeline. Finally, she looked up. "I don't think we should make decisions based on what *could* happen. If the world thought that way, a lot of things would never occur." She held up a palm. "However, I don't want to hurt you. My mate could come knocking on the door any minute, and perhaps I wouldn't be able to do anything about it. Right at the moment though, that seems slim."

"The urge to be with a mate is intense and often beyond our control."

Chelsea set down her bottle and sat up straighter. "What are you really trying to say? That you want to walk away now?"

"No! I just think we need to cool it for a while. Maybe we could go two days without seeing each other. After that, I'm game for taking in a movie or going bowling or something to see if we can be together without tearing off each other's clothes."

She laughed. "Do you even know how to bowl?"

That was what she took away from his discussion? It probably didn't matter. "No, I don't, but it's what people who date do. We are not mates, and as such should be able to go on an ordinary date without having sex."

Once more, she held up a palm. "You just said you only wanted sex. Now you're sending me mixed signals."

Damn. Declan was always decisive. It was why he was a good businessman. "I'm sorry. I'd say it's all your fault, but I don't like to blame others. You excite me like no one ever has. Can we do this my way, please?"

"Fine. Just so you know, I like you too, Declan Sinclair. A lot. I would love to spend more time with you, but I will let you decide on how much time we spend together. If what you say is true, once my mate walks in the proverbial door, then I won't give you a second look, right?"

He leaned closer and twirled her blonde hair between his fingers. "I hope you'd at least look back over your shoulder."

She smiled. "I promise I will never, ever forget you—even if I move back to Earth."

Earth. It might only be a portal jump away, but that was too far for him. When Chelsea moved within kissing distance, his dragon roared, and his scales glowed. Damn it.

Declan cleared his throat. "Ready for your grand tour?"

She slapped her thighs and stood. "Show me everything."

When she dragged her gaze down his body, Declan had to look away. He wished like hell he understood these conflicting feelings. Stupid dragon must be rebelling against him for not finding anyone else to care for these last three years.

TWO DAYS! CHELSEA had been going crazy—or maybe it was her wolf that was almost out of control without Declan. Once, when Chelsea was traveling between the condo and the cabin, she ran into Finn, who happened to mention that Declan was in one foul mood. As much as she disliked herself for it, it took effort not to smile. It meant she wasn't the only one suffering.

Moving into her own place had been exciting, but it would have been a lot nicer if Declan had been there to give her some recommendations on where she could buy a few things.

Stop lying, her wolf shouted.

Fine, it would have been nice to take a break every now and again, but I want him here for a few other reasons too. Living in the woods was a new adventure and sharing it with someone she cared about would make it that much more enjoyable.

Throughout the move, Chelsea would repeat their conversation about why they needed to take a break from each other. Unfortunately, she came to the same conclusion Declan had. It would be better if they kept their distance, at least for a few days. But hadn't he said only two days?

Tomorrow, she'd have to go back to work, which would hopefully take her mind off the situation. She dropped down onto the sofa, her muscles tired from all the moving. Mentally, she went through what she'd have to do after work. The first order of business was grocery shopping. The immediate problem was that the gas tank was banging empty, and she had no idea where to fill up. She'd actually searched the car for a place to put the gas—or whatever fuel the car used—but she'd failed to find anything that resembled a nozzle entry point.

She wanted to call Declan, but he might feel obligated to leave the mine and help her. Making more work for him was the last thing she wanted. No, her best chance of making it to the shelter tomorrow and then having enough gas to go shopping afterward would be to drive to Finn's bar now and ask him. After all, it was his car. Chelsea was sure her twin wouldn't mind a little distraction while at work.

She smiled. Back in the States, if she had a particularly rough day, she'd drive to McKinnon's Pub and Pool and shoot the breeze with Finn if he wasn't too busy. He always made her feel better, so why not visit him at The Wing's Bar? He'd mentioned how incredible the food was there, and she could use a relaxing meal.

With more pep in her step, she left, hoping the car didn't run out of gas before she reached town. The dirt road leading from her cabin to the main road was a bit spooky at night, so she locked her car doors. If she'd been back in Tennessee, she wouldn't have bothered.

To be honest, what resided on Tarradon kind of intimidated her. Sure, there were the usual shifters, like wolves and bears, but what else was out there? She was learning about new species all the time. At least if she bumped into a dragon, she could run into the woods where he most likely wouldn't follow.

Before she let her fears get to her, she neared town. Three minutes later, Chelsea was passing the bar where Finn worked. Finding a parking place wasn't easy, but eventually, she located one two blocks away. More and more she realized she was not a big city person. Give her the countryside any day.

Making certain to keep an eye out for anything out of the ordinary, she strode toward The Wing's Bar. She still wasn't used to the ways of Tarradon, but as soon as she stepped inside, her muscles relaxed. The music was festive, and the flashing lights over the bar gave it a cheerful ambiance. Wanting to talk to Finn, Chelsea headed to the bar—which took some doing.

A ton of people were crammed into the small space. Many were shifters, though she couldn't tell what kind. From their size, she bet the majority were dragon shifters. Finn had told her that Declan spent most of his waking hours at the mine, so she was quite confident she wouldn't run into him there.

A rather loud, piercing laugh drew her attention to the corner of the room. Chelsea spun around and spotted a tall woman with long, black hair resting a hip on a table. She was leaning over some guy stroking his face. The woman turned her head, forcing Chelsea to blink. It was Sabrina. Holy shit.

Because it was none of her business what Sabrina did, Chelsea shook her head and continued to make her way to Finn. She had no idea so many people liked to drink on a Sunday night.

When she reached him, Finn had his palms on the counter talking with someone. He laughed, and her heart blossomed. He really seemed to have found his spot. She slipped onto a stool and waited to flag his attention.

He must have sensed her, for he looked her way a moment later. The double take was expected, but it still delighted her. He excused himself from the man he was chatting with and came over to her.

"To what do I owe the pleasure? Or are you looking to drown your sorrows?"

Did she look sad? Sure, she was a bit out of sorts, but how could he tell? "I actually came because your car is almost out of gas, or whatever it uses for fuel, and I need to figure out how to fill it up."

He chuckled. "That is tricky. Kaleena had to explain it to me the first time too. We use gas, but the stations here are different. How about I show you tomorrow, and then we can set up a bank account for you, so you can pay for the gas."

"Thanks, but I might run out before tomorrow."

Finn looked over his shoulder. "That bad, huh?"

"It's on fumes."

"Then let's fill it up for you right now. You can come with me, and I can show you what to do."

"You don't have to do that. You're working. Plus, I'm starving."

"Okay, we'll get you something to eat first. I'm due for a break in a half hour anyway. I'll drive you over and show you how to fill up. How does that sound?"

She smiled. "You are the best brother."

"Don't let the rest of the family hear you say that." He grinned then tapped her nose. "What would you like to eat?"

"What do you have?" she asked. Finn rattled off some bar food options, and they all sounded good. "I'll go with a hamburger and fries."

"Good choice. And to drink?"

"A beer."

"Coming right up."

Her back was to the main crowd, but her wolf was acting up for some reason. Random bolts of lust and excitement kept poking her, which was ridiculous on so many levels.

Will you stop it! She couldn't help but chastise her wolf.

If you would turn around, you'd see your mate. On second thought, don't.

What the hell did that mean? Naturally, Chelsea had to swivel back around. For some reason, her gaze shot to where Sabrina was plastered to her man. When her boss' sister broke the kiss, exposing the man's face, Chelsea nearly fell off her stool.

Declan? What was he doing here? And kissing Sabrina no less? As if she'd willed him to see her, his gaze caught hers and all joy evaporated from his face.

He said something to Sabrina, stood, and plowed his way over to her.

"What are you doing here?" he asked a few seconds later. He sounded accusatory, like she had no right to leave her cabin.

"For your information, my car was about to run out of gas, and I needed to find out how to fill it. I came to ask Finn." She lifted her chin.

"You could have called me."

That was rich. "I thought you'd be busy at the mine. I also didn't want to bother you, especially since you said we needed time to cool off. I just didn't realize *cool off* to you meant you'd take the opportunity to have a *date with someone else!*"

He held up a hand. "I did not have a date with Sabrina. Griffin is in charge of sales for our mine, but since he was busy, he asked me to speak with one of our best customers about buying some of our metals. The man insisted I meet him here. As I was about to leave, Sabrina showed up."

That sounded plausible. "How do you know her? Or does everyone around here know the Sinclairs?" There was no reason for her heart to be beating so fast or her palms to be sweating, but they were.

"Sabrina and I used to date." She wasn't able to tell if his locked gaze held defiance or cheer.

It took all of Chelsea's resolve to school her emotions. "Used to?"

His brows pinched, and then he leaned closer. "Do you think I'd make love with you and go out with Sabrina two days later?"

She huffed out a laugh. "We never mentioned anything about being exclusive."

Before he could comment, Sabrina strode up to Declan. She dragged a hand down his shoulder and gave him what Chelsea could only describe as her sexiest look. "Come on, sweetie. It's lonely at the table."

Declan's jaw clenched. Not wanting to interfere in his love life, Chelsea held up a hand. "You go ahead. I'm grabbing a bite, and then Finn is driving me to the gas station."

Sabrina tugged on his arm. "Lover?"

Chelsea couldn't handle seeing them together. It made her sick. She'd just swiveled around on her seat when Declan placed a hand on her shoulder. "We'll talk later."

At the moment, she wasn't in the mood to speak with him—ever.

Someone other than Finn set a beer in front of her. "Your food will be up in a moment."

She tried to smile and thank the young man, but her lips were quivering too much. When she lifted her beer, her hand trembled so much, liquid sloshed out of the sides. Damn Declan. No, they weren't fated for each other, but the pain of him being with someone else didn't hurt any less.

She'd gulped down half her drink when Finn came over carrying her dinner. "What was that all about?"

"What was what all about?"

He cocked a head. "Declan. I thought you two were chummy."

"Past tense."

"Ouch."

She inhaled deeply. "Did you know that he used to date Sabrina?"

Finn shook his head. "It was probably before I arrived."

That meant their time together was in the past. "It sure looks like Sabrina at least wants to pick up where they left off." Her words came out bitter, and she shouldn't act that way. She and Declan could still have sex—and only sex. Too bad her heart wanted more.

Finn cupped her hand. "Is that so bad? Declan isn't your mate. Maybe you should go about your job and wait for Mr. Right to come knocking."

The problem was that Chelsea's wolf was still convinced Declan was Mr. Right.

Chapter Eleven

AS SOON AS Chelsea left with Finn, Declan excused himself.

Sabrina reached out and grabbed his arm. "You don't have to go, do you? Come back to my place. I can show you a good time. For old times' sake?"

Seriously? He'd told Sabrina several times already that what they had was temporary and that he wasn't looking for anything other than some fun. She had been completely on board at the time, but when she started to get serious and look for commitment, he had ended it.

"Sabrina, we had this discussion already. We can be friends, but nothing else is going to happen."

Sabrina scooted out of the booth. "Then will you walk me to my car?"

It was the least he could do—especially in front of a bar at night. "Sure."

She slipped her arm through his, and his dragon cringed at the contact. He wanted to remove her hand, but he didn't want to cause a scene, so he'd let her cling to him until they reached her vehicle.

Once she opened the door, Sabrina slipped in, and Declan leaned an arm on the hood. "Listen, Sabrina."

She held up a hand. "Don't think about brushing me off. We are right for each other. Remember what you said? No strings attached. Just a good time in bed. And I'm good with that now."

He didn't need this. He didn't want to be a dick, but she just wasn't getting it. "Look, I'm just not interested anymore."

"It's Chelsea, isn't it? I saw the way you looked at her."

He had no idea how to answer that, nor did he want to. "You know my reasons why I ended things."

"I understand that you thought I was looking for more, but I'm only suggesting we have fun together."

At one time, he would have said to hell with it and jumped at what she was offering, but he couldn't bring himself to do it. He wanted Chelsea and that was all. "I'm sorry, Sabrina, but I just don't have the feelings for you that you want me to. Take care of yourself, and drive safely."

He stepped back and closed her door. Once she drove off, he decided he either needed a Chelsea fix or therapy. Since Chelsea had been rather cold toward him tonight after seeing Sabrina kiss him, he decided to ask for some advice.

Instead of driving, he walked to the end of town and took flight.

A few minutes later, he arrived at the Four Sisters Pottery store. It was dark inside, but it made sense since the store was closed.

He rang the bell and waited. A minute later, lights lit up the back room, and Magnolia came out to greet him. While he had no idea how old these women were, Magnolia seemed to be the matriarch of the group—and the strictest one.

The store lights blazed, and a second later, she was ushering him in. "Declan, this is a surprise. What can I do for you?"

While he had rehearsed what he wanted to say, the words now escaped him. "I kind of have a problem."

"What kind of problem?"

He wasn't about to tell the prim and proper Magnolia that he'd had the most amazing sexual experience with a woman, and that he couldn't stop thinking about her. Furthermore, it was with a woman who wasn't his mate. "Do you recall that my mate, Bess, was killed three years back?"

Magnolia wrapped an arm around his shoulder and led him to the back room. Potters' wheels took up most of the space, but in the corner sat a table and four chairs. "Of course I do. Have a seat so we can chat. Can I get you some coffee?"

"I'd love some, thanks." He needed something to do with his hands.

While she fixed him a cup, Declan tried to figure out the best way to word his question.

Magnolia delivered the steaming brew for both of them, and then sat across from him. "You're confused, I see."

Whether she was a psychic or a goddess, he didn't know, but his whole family had come to accept the sisters' talents as impressive. "Yes." He sipped his hot drink. "Do you know if it is possible to have a second chance at a mate?"

Her eyes widened, and his heart sunk. "I've never heard of any such thing, but neither my sisters nor I have control over Fate. Have you met someone?"

If they didn't have control over Fate, why were they called the Four Sisters of Fate. "Yes. She's Finn McKinnon's twin sister."

"From Earth?"

"Yes, but she's here now."

"I see. And you are highly attracted to her."

"Very much so." He could tell himself until the moon disappeared that he only wanted her for sex, but the futility of believing it had finally become clear. He wanted more, whatever that meant.

Magnolia stared off into space for a moment. "Didn't Bess come from Earth?"

She sounded like Birk. "Yes."

She snapped her fingers. "Ophelia mentioned that she was taking you back to Earth to help heal someone. Is that where you met Chelsea?"

How did she know Ophelia, and how did she know Chelsea's name? Perhaps Finn had mentioned her. Too many other questions bombarded him, but he needed to remain focused. "Yes, but before you ask, Chelsea looks nothing like Bess."

"I was about to ask that. I wish I could help you, but there is no potion in the world that can change Fate. The rule says one man or woman—one mate."

He figured she'd say that, but he had to ask. "Thanks for letting me vent."

Declan pushed back his chair. Uncertain where to dump the remainder of the coffee, he left his cup on the table.

"I'm sorry I couldn't help," Magnolia said. "I'll walk you out."

Once he shifted and took off, instead of heading back to the mine or to his condo, he headed to the mountain where he and Chelsea had watched the stars and made love. Perhaps the memory would bring him closer to her. Right now, a memory might be all he'd have for the rest of his life.

CHELSEA HAD BARELY been able to get through the day, which was unfair to the animals. They hadn't done anything wrong. Declan had. She'd not been her usual affectionate self with them, and they could sense it.

One of the tramors was rather listless. Feeling a bit guilty, she shot into healing mode. Placing her hands on the animal's head, she closed her eyes, listening to what ailed the animal. Ever since she'd arrived on Tarradon, her ability to communicate with animals had increased. She believed that when she embraced her Wendayan side, her powers had steadily grown stronger. If it hadn't been for those blue sparks, she never would have known what she was truly capable of.

Waves of fear, pain, and then some joy entered her mind. The animal complained that his side hurt. Chelsea wasn't sure which side, so she gently ran her hands down both of his flanks. When she hit one particular spot, the animal whimpered. Upon closer perusal, she found a large bruise. It was possible this tramor ran into something. It was also possible that Stick or Marty had kicked him. Anger ripped through her at that thought, though she wouldn't accuse either of them without proof.

Chelsea could heal animals, but it took a lot out of her. Right now, she didn't care. It would bring her joy knowing she'd done some good.

"Lie down on your side," she said, as she guided the animal to stretch out.

Once he was in position, she ran her hands along his flank, sending her healing magic into him. His heartbeat slowed, and his muscles relaxed. It didn't take long before the animal was back on its feet. He licked her hands and then her face. She laughed. "If you can help it, stay away from whoever hurt you."

As if the tramor understood, he let out what sounded like a cross between a howl and a bark, and then trotted off.

Chelsea stood. Weak from the experience, she spent the rest of the day alternating between paperwork, making phone calls to people interested in adopting, and feeding the animals. By closing time, she was more than ready for a run. While her physical energy had returned, her mental energy remained low. She just couldn't shake witnessing that kiss between Sabrina and Declan.

After she said goodbye to Stick and the animals, she took off. Chelsea debated stopping at the store for food, but her need for release had to come first. Once she drove home, she rushed inside, ditched her clothes, and raced outside. How wonderful to be in a place where the weather was never cold. Sure, she'd missed running around in the snow, but the balmy weather spoke to her more.

Once she shifted, she took off down her usual path. The adrenaline rush from being outside usually helped calm her wolf. When she was in a contemplative mood, like she was today, she liked to sit by water. While the spot near her home didn't have a view of the valley below or the stars above, the sound of the stream would ease the ache in her heart. Hopefully, with enough time and thought, she'd figure out how she wanted to handle Declan.

She inhaled the fresh air as she ran, slowly releasing the tension in her muscles. When she finally slowed and found a spot to relax, she took in the soothing sounds of the forest animals.

After resting for close to an hour by the gurgling brook, she'd decided Declan was the one who needed to take the next step. She didn't want to second-guess what Sabrina meant to him. Not only that, if—and that was a big if—her mate did cross her path, she'd have to go to him and leave Declan. If she and Declan were together for any length of time, his heart would be broken again.

Ugh. Life wasn't fair. To think she'd been so excited when she first thought the two of them belonged together. If only Fate would have been kind enough to give her a sign—before she came here and told her that she had it all wrong—Chelsea wouldn't be in this position.

A clap of thunder sounded, and she rose to her haunches and raced back home, hoping to rid her body and mind of all the worry it had collected. After a quick shower, she changed and headed to the store for food.

Buying for one was always depressing. It hadn't helped that Chelsea had been mentally deciding what cool things she could make Declan for dinner—assuming she could find all the ingredients. Now, there wouldn't be any intimate affair or after dinner romance.

She wanted to punch the depression out of her. Feeling sad for herself never helped anyone. What would help would be chocolate chip cookies with ice cream. Yeah, that was it. With a new mission, she added sweets to her shopping list.

FOR HER OWN mental health, Chelsea decided it would be best not to see Finn or Kaleena since her brother would report on Declan's mood. If she learned he was in a foul mood, she might be tempted to rush over to his place and soothe his aches—as well as quench her needs. If Declan acted like life was wonderful, she'd want to throw up. No, it was better not to know how this little break up was affecting him and just pretend as if her mate would waltz into the shelter looking for some unloved animal to adopt.

She smiled at that image. Yes, for the time being, she'd remain on Tarradon. She'd have to ask Finn to escort her back to Earth one more time to say goodbye properly to her family and friends. She'd tell them that she was convinced she could have a new life on Tarradon. Naturally, trips back to Earth—especially around Christmas—were a must.

For now, Chelsea would go to work, enjoy the animals, and go home. If the girls suggested a night out, she'd go. The best thing right now was not to worry about her love life. She'd explore Tarradon and learn about the culture here. For now, returning to Earth permanently wasn't a good option.

"Chelsea?" Stick strode up to her.

She'd been daydreaming again. She stood. "Yes?"

"Have you fed the new kittens that came in last week?"

No, she hadn't. "That's next on my list."

Crap. The last thing she needed was to be fired for not doing her job. Decision made: no more thoughts about Declan!

Oh, no you don't, her wolf said. *He's our mate.*

You do realize that Tarradon is full of witches, or rather white lighters, who might be able to do a spell to shut you up?

You wouldn't dare, her wolf shot back.

I just might.

After Chelsea tended to the kittens, she was able to get through the day, then the next day, and the next.

On Friday, she was cleaning one of the cages, when a car rolled to a stop in the parking lot. Oh shit. It was Sabrina again. She hadn't shown up all week, and Chelsea had thought she might have been too embarrassed to visit after having made such a fuss over Declan at the bar. Guess not.

Just her luck, Chelsea was cleaning poop from the cages when Sabrina passed her, dressed in a clean white outfit.

"Hey, Chelsea!" Sabrina said with an overly cheerful tone.

"How's it going?" Her response wasn't as upbeat as she'd hoped. Jealousy was an ugly trait, but right now she couldn't help it.

"Fantastic." Sabrina grinned and stepped into the office.

Whatever. If Declan was happy being with her, then so be it. Wallowing in self-pity wouldn't get her anywhere.

For the next few hours, she scrubbed the cages, fed the animals, and talked to each of those who were sheltered there. When the end of her weekday arrived, she was happy to have a few days off. Chelsea was hoping Kaleena or maybe Tory would be available to go out. Yes, she'd told herself that she didn't want to know how Declan was doing but not knowing was driving her crazy.

With as much calm as she could muster, she ducked her head into the boss' office. Of course, Sabrina was there.

"I'm heading out now," Chelsea said. "All of the cages are cleaned and the animals fed."

"See you on Monday," Stick said with little enthusiasm.

Chelsea had the sense his sister had been badmouthing her. What was her problem? Sabrina was the winner here. The dark haired beauty had Declan. Chelsea didn't.

As quickly as she could, Chelsea rushed out to the car and sped home. Being totally smelly and gross, she dumped her clothes in the washing machine, and then jumped into the shower. The hot streaming water felt divine. As much as she wanted to stay in there for an hour, a run would do her wolf a lot of good. After she rubbed her hair more or less dry, she wrapped a towel around her body.

Just as she was drying off, a knock sounded, and from the sudden blast of heat racing through her, she knew who it was.

"Chelsea, it's Declan," he called through the door.

If she took the time to change, he might leave. Decision time— see him or let him go? She inhaled. She'd answer the door semi-covered and tell him she needed a minute to dress.

Or maybe she wouldn't tell him anything at all!

Chapter Twelve

D ECLAN WASN'T SURE if Chelsea would appreciate him stopping by, but he needed to apologize to her. Yes, Sabrina had leaned over and kissed him, but it wasn't as if he wanted her to.

He thought it best to let Chelsea cool down a bit before stopping by, but he probably shouldn't have waited six days. Common sense had told him to keep his distance a little longer, but his dragon had threatened to shift all by himself and fly to the cabin if Declan didn't see her today.

When she didn't answer, he knocked again. "Please open up, Chels."

Footsteps sounded, and when she opened the door, a vision stood before him. Her blonde hair was wet and tangled around her shoulders. That alone was enough to send his dragon into a fiery expression of total lust, but to see that cinnamon colored towel barely covering her breasts had Declan almost panting.

Her eyes glowed amber as she ran her gaze from his face to his crotch. When several sparks shot off her body, Declan stepped inside, his gaze never leaving her face. If he drank in any more of her, he wasn't sure what he'd do.

"What are you doing here, Declan? I thought you were with Sabrina now."

Damn. From the way her eyes were glowing, how her eyeteeth had sharpened, and the fact sparks were firing rapidly off her body, her wolf certainly was happy to see him. He just couldn't be sure what Chelsea wanted. "I am not with Sabrina. She came onto me. I just stopped by to explain to you what happened and to apologize. I didn't handle things well."

Chelsea planted her hands on her hips, and the towel slipped a little. "It's been a week. You could have called if what I saw wasn't the two of you getting back together."

"I wanted to give you some space."

"Space for what?" She stood straighter.

He stabbed a hand over his head. "Fuck."

Chelsea took a step toward him and tilted up her chin. "Fuck what? Fuck me? Fuck you? Or just plain fuck."

The way she said fuck had him chuckling. "You are something else, Chelsea McKinnon. Can we start over again?" *Please say yes.*

"I don't understand."

Why was she making this so hard?

Because you decided to let her get away, his dragon spit out.

It was the best for both of us. Or so he kept telling himself.

"Can we sit down and talk?" he asked.

"Let me change." When she turned around, half exposing her butt, something inside him made him reach out for her arm, but he missed and ended up grabbing the towel instead.

"Holy shit," he whispered, as he stood there holding the towel, staring at her now completely naked body. The urge to kiss her was so intense all rational thoughts became blocked. He probably shouldn't touch her or hold her, but he couldn't help it. "Chel-sea."

A second later, she was in his arms with their lips pressed together. Desperation overwhelmed him. Why had Declan believed he could stay away from her? Every cell in his body lit up, many flashing red.

Seconds later, Declan realized he still had the towel in his one hand and dropped it just as Chelsea lifted her arms around his neck.

That did it. He just crossed the point of no return. His dragon licked and kicked, too excited to ever calm down unless he tasted her. He gathered her damp hair in his fist and tugged, loving how it made him feel whole again.

With the flat of his hand, he ran his palm down her curvy back, and over her slightly wet skin, which was slick and delicious. Every touch ignited him. As if Fate commanded him to be with her, Declan edged her a few feet to the sofa, swung her around, and sat her on the arm.

"You have no idea what you do to me."

She held out her arms, both of which were shooting blue sparks everywhere. "I think it's evident what you're doing to me."

Declan nodded. "I know I said we needed to keep our distance, and that our relationship should just be about sex, but I can't stop myself from wanting you, needing you. Chelsea. I have to be with you. Even I don't understand why or how it happened, but it did."

Reaching behind her, Chelsea planted her palms on the seat and widened her legs in invitation. "So what's stopping you from taking what you want?"

Declan's hands turned into claws, and Chelsea smiled. She'd forgiven him! Or so he believed. Inhaling to calm his inner animal, his claws retracted. Sometimes, he wanted to beat his beast. He'd lose, but it would be worth trying.

"Nothing." Declan dropped to his knees, spread her legs wide, and swiped his tongue across her opening. His intention was to excite her, but instead, her scent nearly did him in.

Chelsea gasped. "That feels so good."

Pleased she seemed to want this as much as he did, Declan reached up and massaged a breast. Chelsea was everything he wanted in a woman—and partner. If they couldn't mate, they could at least enjoy each other for a long time.

He didn't need to be thinking about the future at the moment but rather how to please her. When he swirled his tongue across her tiny nub and then pressed on her nipple, she sat up and clutched his shoulders. The pressure and rapid breathing meant she was just as much on edge as he was.

"How about a little reciprocation?" Chelsea panted.

Given how much he enjoyed tasting her, it was only fair. He rocked back onto his heels and stood. "I imagine it will be more enjoyable if we are both naked."

"You could say that." She grinned, and his heart swelled.

Almost as fast as he could shift, Declan's clothes soon littered the floor. She whistled and grabbed his hips. Leaning over, she nearly swallowed him whole. Words defied the powerful surge shooting through his veins. He might be able to close his eyes to block out the vision of her, but he couldn't shut off her incredible scent, which seemed to be a combination of peaches and lavender.

Every lick and swirl transported him closer to his climax, something he wanted to avoid at the moment. He gathered her hair in one hand and lifted it out of the way.

Declan would have let her have her fill, but when she grabbed his balls and squeezed, some of his cum released, forcing him to step back. "That's all I can handle."

Before she had any other ideas, he pulled her to her feet, turned her around so she faced the sofa arm, and pressed on her back. It was when she wiggled her butt at him that he almost lost it.

CHELSEA COULDN'T COMPREHEND how willing Declan was to make love with her when he'd basically ignored her for a week, but she certainly wasn't going to complain. From the way he planted his hands on her breasts, leaned over, and nuzzled her neck, he wanted her a lot. Of course, his flashing teal eyes and glowing scales gave it away too.

He ran his hands from her tits to her waist and squeezed. "You excite me like no other," he whispered.

"Show me."

She wasn't normally so bold, but she couldn't help herself when Declan came anywhere near her.

He slipped his cock into her opening and remained still, as if he was working hard not to explode. She, however, didn't have such control. Pressing her hips back, she engulfed most of him. Whoa.

Shards of bliss and rampant lust grabbed her insides and set her on fire. Sucking in a large breath, she waited for the stretching to subside.

When she relaxed, Declan edged into her all the way. His hands returned to her nipples, twisting, pressing, and loving them hard, making her whole body ready to explode with need and desire.

"Yes, Declan, yes." Or at least that was what she meant to say. Her words came out a bit garbled.

He dropped his lips to her neck again, and she stiffened. Biting her would do nothing, and might even hurt if they weren't mates.

Damn Fate.

If Fate were a person, she'd have a serious talk with her. Or him.

When Declan withdrew and drove into her again, all thoughts of revenge against Fate evaporated. Lowering her head and planting her hands on the sofa cushion, she reveled in the glory of each thrust.

Sparks flew, and she soared. When he lowered a hand and reached under her to press on her clit, Chelsea lost it. Her wolf howled while she yelled. Declan's other hand flattened on her stomach as he pummeled his seed into her.

Their breaths ragged, he wrapped his arms around her and kissed her neck. A full minute later, Declan withdrew and then patted her butt. "Be right back."

"I'm not going anywhere." Chelsea dropped to her stomach onto the sofa arm, exhaustion overcoming her.

Declan returned and chuckled. He wiped her clean with the cloth. "How about putting on some clothes so we can talk? If you're naked, we might be repeating this again."

Chelsea drew on all of her strength to get up. Her gaze latched onto his dick, which was standing at attention. "How come your cock is still hard when I'm spent?" She watched Declan's gaze travel over her whole body.

When his eyes met hers, he raised an eyebrow at her. "You keep me that way. Now, if you don't get moving, I will find my way into you again."

"Okay, okay. I'm going." As she sashayed away, she tossed a look back over her shoulder. "Although that's not really a threat, ya know!" Chelsea winked at him.

Chelsea put on some clothes, and when she returned, Declan was dressed and sitting on the sofa. She hoped he hadn't come over to deliver bad news.

Chelsea plopped down next to him. "Can I get you something to drink?"

Declan cupped her face. "I'm good for now. You filled me up."

She loved it when he talked sexy like that. The problem was that it made her fall for him all the more. "Did you stop by for a booty call?" Shit. The second those words came out, she realized her mistake. "I didn't mean it like that. After all, I was the one who practically attacked you."

He ran a knuckle down her cheek. "No, as I told you, I stopped by to apologize for not controlling Sabrina. She can be a tad aggressive. I tried to explain to her that I wasn't interested, but she wouldn't take no for an answer."

"You two were laughing. I heard you."

"You heard Sabrina. I was trying to be nice, but apparently, she didn't get the hint."

He sounded sincere. "So, it's over between you?"

"It never really started, but yes, it's over."

"Then why did you wait a week to come over?" She hadn't meant to sound hurt, but she couldn't help it.

"Like I said, I thought the reception would be lukewarm at best."

She had to think about that. "Okay, I can accept that."

Declan lifted a still damp strand of hair and twirled it in his fingers. "What do we do now? I know we said we'd take a break, but I can't stay away from you."

She smiled, trying to act brave. "I see no reason why we have to. I want you. You want me. How about seeing where things go?" Chelsea held her breath, hoping he'd agree.

He leaned closer. "I don't think we have a choice. We are both animals."

She laughed. "I hope it's the human part of you who wants me."

"There's no doubt about it."

Chapter Thirteen

THE NEXT DAY at work was sunny and full of hope. Most of the animals seemed happy and healthy, and the cages she'd recently cleaned more or less remained that way. Chelsea gathered the two tramors who appeared in need of exercise and led them to the fenced off area to let them run. Even though she hadn't been working at the shelter long, she couldn't help but name these two. One she called Motley, because his fur still had some patches that needed to grow in, and the other was Spot because of the random black and white spots on his brown body. He at least had recovered nicely from whatever had happened to him.

While the animals ran around and played, she leaned against the fence to watch them. Their carefree attitude was so refreshing and loving. Yes. Loving. She couldn't get that word out of her head. Why? Because her thoughts had become consumed with Declan and how he had wormed his way into the depths of her soul.

She sighed. He'd spent last night in her bed and had left early this morning. After falling asleep the first time for an hour, they made love again, slow and sensual. It had been oh, so wonderful.

And that was the problem.

It wasn't so much that she was worried Declan would grow tired of her, but that what he said would come true: her mate would waltz into her life and want her for himself. If she had to choose right now, she would take Declan, making that other man live a lonely life.

Ugh. As she twisted away from the fence, her stomach contracted, causing a wave of nausea to well up. What the hell? The last two mornings she'd been ill, but thankfully the discomfort had passed quickly.

Not wanting to be sick in the open, Chelsea made sure the animals were content before rushing back to the office. Stick must be in the back because she didn't see him. Marty had taken off earlier in the day and had yet to return.

Just in time, Chelsea made it to the bathroom and vomited. She searched her mind for what she'd eaten and decided it must have been the cheese. It had looked a little suspect. The alternative couldn't exist. A month before she'd arrived in Tarradon, she'd taken a shot to prevent pregnancy that was designed to last three months.

Not that she didn't yearn for children—she did—but that honor was reserved for once she found her mate. Declan had told her numerous time he wasn't the one.

After washing her hands and rinsing out her mouth, she stepped into the hallway. Oh, shit. Just who she didn't need to run into.

"Hello, Chelsea." Sabrina's brows pinched together. "Are you all right?"

Chelsea looked down to see if some piece of food was caught in her hair or had landed on her shirt, but she didn't spot anything. "I ate something bad last night."

Sabrina rubbed her arm. "I have some anti-nausea pills if you need any."

Chelsea forced a smile. "Thanks, but I feel much better now." Not really, but she wasn't about to confide in her—especially since she was Declan's ex-girlfriend. "If you'll excuse me, I left the two feisty tramors running around in the pen. I need to check on them."

"Sure."

As soon as Chelsea stepped outside, she inhaled deeply. Even though Declan claimed he had no interest in that woman anymore, there was something creepy and insincere about her. Whatever. Chelsea had animals to feed and two tramors to return to their cages.

While she was rounding them up, she caught site of Sabrina leaving after a very short visit. Good riddance. As if the gods had witnessed the exchange, Chelsea's cell rang. When she checked the screen, she smiled.

"Hey, Declan. Miss me?"

He laughed. "Always. Say listen, I'm sorry but I can't stop by tonight. Many of the Guardians are heading out now to combat some fires plaguing the farmers on the edge of the province. We need to find out who is setting these blazes. That means I probably won't be back before late tonight."

She held in her disappointment. "I understand. Heroes have to do hero things." He laughed, just as she had hoped. "Will I see you tomorrow then?"

"Let's hope. Thane's calling. Gotta go."

"Bye."

Even though the conversation was short, hearing Declan's voice had boosted her spirits. In fact, it helped make the rest of the afternoon fly by. When it was time to leave, she punched out, jumped in her car, and took off. Normally, she would have headed home for a run, but she wanted to put that niggling idea to rest. Instead of taking a right at the end of the long dirt road to her cabin, she turned left toward town.

Once on the outskirts, she parked and went into the pharmacy where she purchased a pregnancy test. She felt a little foolish since the shot was supposed to work, but maybe it was a defective batch or something. Taking the test would eliminate any doubt.

After buying the test, she stopped in Angelique's Coffee Shop. A good mocha cappuccino and a sweet roll was just what she needed. If she couldn't see Declan tonight, then these little bits of sweet pleasure would have to do.

The shop was practically empty. Without all the chatter, the soft music and muted colors provided a calming atmosphere. On the far wall was a glass counter filled with all kinds of pastries, as well as croissants and snacks. Comfy tub chairs clustered together on one side of the room with coffee tables scattered between them. Booths and a few tables were on the other side. All in all, the coffee shop was very homey.

Chelsea had only been in here once before with Kaleena who was friends with the owner. At the counter, Chelsea placed her order and then sat in one of the booths that overlooked the street. Being able to relax and do nothing helped calm her. Five minutes later, the owner came over with Chelsea's order, placed it in front of her, and then slid into the booth across from her.

"Hi, I'm Angelique. I believe you came in with Kaleena once."

Her memory was impressive. "Yes. She's mated to Finn; he's my twin."

"Ah, yes, I remember now." Angelique was tall and thin with pale blonde hair and even whiter skin. She had an ethereal beauty about her. It might have been the early evening light coming through the window, but a glow appeared around her head, making it look as if she wore a halo.

Chelsea had never seen anyone quite like her before. Her gaze was even a bit unsettling, like she could see right through a person.

"Something is troubling you," Angelique said with confidence.

Chelsea forced a smile and said, "Nothing that a delicious cup of coffee and a pastry won't cure."

Angelique returned a genuine smile. "That's good to hear. If I remember correctly, Kaleena said you're working at an animal shelter."

"Yes." They chatted a bit about what she did, but Angelique didn't seem all that interested in the details.

"Let me know if I'm too nosey, but I get the sense that something happened today to unsettle you," Angelique said.

Was this woman some kind of psychic? Nothing would surprise her on Tarradon. Psychic or not, Angelique couldn't know anything about her being sick this morning. "Nothing other than the ex-girlfriend of the man I like stopped by." She wrinkled her nose. "I don't care for her in the least."

Her eyes widened. "Ooh. I can see why. That must have been awkward. Was she snippy because you are now dating her ex?"

"Not really, but there is no love lost between us. I really, really like this guy. He's Kaleena's brother."

"Ah, yes. Declan. I've seen him. Quite the hottie."

Heat raced up her face. "I agree, but therein lies the problem."
Angelique's brows rose. Given how interested she seemed, Chelsea
decided to tell her more and ask for her unbiased opinion. "You see,
we aren't mates."

"Oh. And you're worried if and when your mate shows up, you
might not want to be with him."

"Exactly." How did the woman know just what to say? Chelsea
explained that Declan had a mate, but that she'd passed.

Chelsea wasn't sure why she felt compelled to tell this stranger
her life's story, but Angelique gave her such a calming and safe
feeling that Chelsea just found herself sharing.

Angelique glanced around the shop before leaning forward. "In
my experience, I've learned to take one day at a time. Enjoy him
while you can. Life is too short."

There were those words again. She liked this woman. "I couldn't
agree more."

Just then, four customers piled into the store, and Angelique slid
out of the booth. "Be happy and have fun."

This time, Chelsea's smile came out genuine. "I will and thank
you."

After Angelique greeted her customers, Chelsea took her time
savoring the richness of the coffee and the sweetness of the pastry,
dreaming about what she wanted to do with Declan the next time
they were together. Being surrounded by the excitement of city life
was beginning to grow on her. She could see why Finn loved it here.

The coffee shop started to fill up. Not wanting to take up a
whole booth to herself, Chelsea finished up and vacated her spot to
head home. Most likely she was procrastinating because she didn't
want to find out if she was pregnant—as unlikely a scenario as it was.

Once in the cabin, she understood she wouldn't rest until she
checked. It only took a minute, but she must have stared at the
results for ten. She was pregnant. Disbelief mixed with anger at

herself for not being more careful. The timing was just plain bad. Had she been on Earth, she would have marched into her doctor's office and asked for an explanation. Then she would have called her mom and listened to how being pregnant was one of the greatest joys in life. At the moment, she wasn't buying it, but eventually she might.

Suddenly, it hit really hit her that she was pregnant and with someone who wasn't her mate. Could Fate be any crueler? Shit!

The hardest part was figuring out how to tell Declan and not having her mom around to help her through this. For a few seconds, she debated asking Finn to take her back to Earth, but that wouldn't be fair to Declan. As the father, he had the right to decide where they should go from there.

Chelsea was about to grab a bottle of wine, only to realize that water or juice would be her drink of choice from now on. Her life was about to change—and she hoped for the better.

THE NEXT MORNING at work, Chelsea became sick once more, but this time she'd learned her lesson. She worked close to the building so she wouldn't be too far from the facilities. She'd also stashed a spare set of clothes in her car in case she made a mess.

As Chelsea was gathering some food from a bin at the side of the building to feed the animals, she noticed Stick rounding the corner. "Hey Chelsea, I just got an emergency call. Do you think you can handle whatever comes up? I shouldn't be gone more than an hour."

"Sure. No problem." From the way his gaze was shifting from right to left, something bad had happened. "Is everything okay?"

"I'm not sure. Marty called and says he needs help with something. I'll be back as quickly as I can. Call if you need anything."

She smiled, trying to look as innocent as possible. "Will do."

The moment Stick pulled out, she dashed inside. The few times when Chelsea had to speak with Stick about something, he'd been very secretive about what went on in the back room. Sure, his office was in the rear, but she had the sense he was hiding something. Could it be stolen animals that he only showed to his special clients, or was it something more sinister? Perhaps it was her hormones interfering with her thoughts, but Stick was an odd duck that she didn't trust.

Fearing her boss would change his mind and come back sooner than he'd said, she headed to the rear. When she twisted the office knob, it was locked. Damn. However, having grown up around a sea of brothers had its benefits. Her dad was in the security business and had taught all of them some tricks of the trade—the first being how to pick a lock.

She rushed to the front, located two paper clips, and returned. The lock looked similar but not identical to that on Earth, but it didn't take her long to figure it out. After a little fiddling, the door popped open.

Chelsea stepped inside and was immediately disappointed. It looked like an ordinary office, complete with a lone file cabinet and a desk with a lot of junk on top. Behind the desk sat a door, which was an odd location for one.

She walked around the small space, trying to decide if her imagination was out of control. The answer? Yes.

As she headed out, a whine filtered through that odd-placed door. Aha! Chelsea turned around. As she edged closer, a wave of shifter signatures hit her all at once. What the hell?

Pressing her ear to the door, she heard multiple grunts and growls. She grabbed the handle and yanked. Of course, this door was locked too. Unfortunately, it didn't have an ordinary lock. She'd need a key to open it. Even though she didn't expect to find one, she pulled open each desk drawer and carefully looked for one. In the back of the third drawer sat a set of keys.

With trembling fingers, she tested each one until the fourth key did the trick. Slowly, Chelsea opened the door. Not only was the inside pitch black, but the smell overpowered her. From the stench and shifter signatures, someone was there. She ran her hand along the side of the wall until she found a switch. When she flicked on the overhead light, her heart broke.

Along the back wall were ten cages, each containing a wolf or some other small animal. Around each of their necks was a silver collar, similar to what Kaleena said she had been forced to wear around her wrists when she'd been held captive by the Royals.

"If any of you can understand me, I'll try to find a way to free you." She doubted they could shift and survive. The collar would choke them.

Sounds of tires crunching on the driveway jerked her attention away from the dilemma. Was Stick returning? Shit!

She flipped off the lights, closed and locked the door, and then shoved the keys back into the drawer. Too bad the odor from the other room lingered in his office. Damn. It was too late to do anything about that.

As fast as she could, she locked his door and rushed down the hall. Through the glass front door, she spotted Stick's truck. Had he forgotten something?

Not wanting to be seen, she ducked into the bathroom and hid in the stall. Footsteps sounded. Once he passed by, she flushed the toilet, and then washed her hands, waiting until her blood pressure dropped a little. With her head held high, she left the bathroom.

Without glancing at Stick's office, she took a step toward the front door when he called to her. "Chelsea?"

Chapter Fourteen

CHELSEA SPUN AROUND and painted on a look of surprise at her boss. "You're back! That didn't take as long as you thought. I take it everything turned out well?"

"Yes. Marty overreacted. I wasn't needed after all."

"Great!"

"No problems here?" he asked, his gaze searching her face.

Sweat pooled under her arms. "Nope. No one showed up. I'm just going to take my break. I have a snack in my car." She strode out of there, holding her breath the whole time.

As soon as the door closed behind her, she exhaled. Oh, shit. Oh, shit. She eyed her car, debating if she should leave now or wait. If she drove off now though, Stick would know something was up. He'd chase her down—assuming he figured out that she'd discovered his secret. What that secret was exactly, she didn't know. It *could* be innocent, though she doubted it. Putting regular animals in quarantine was one thing, but at least two of them were shifters— and both Marty and Stick would have known that.

No, the best thing to do was act natural—and call Declan as soon as she could. Hopefully, he wouldn't be in his animal form and could answer. Fighting fires didn't seem to be a dragon thing, so he probably hadn't shifted.

She sat in her car for her fifteen-minute break since that was what she had told Stick she'd be doing. Once her time was up, Chelsea went back to work. Thankfully, she had plenty to keep her busy. She finished feeding the animals and then raked out some of the pens. When Stick didn't come stomping out, she decided it was safe to call Declan. Or should she wait to contact him? She certainly didn't need his big dragon self to leave his Guardian duties just to snoop around. What if nothing was seriously wrong? She'd lose her job over nothing. Yikes.

Kaleena, on the other hand, would be more levelheaded. She would contact the right people to investigate quietly. Making sure that Stick wasn't near, she slipped out her phone and called her. Kaleena answered on the third ring.

"Chelsea, this is a surprise."

"I only have a minute," she whispered. "I saw something that I don't think I was supposed to."

"Are you in danger?" Her tone went from cheerful to serious in a flash.

Probably. "Not right now."

Chelsea explained about the cages in the back, the silver collars, and the shifter signatures.

"Shit. That sounds like the Royals are involved in this. I'll call my father and see what he wants to do. Whatever you do, don't call Declan. Knowing him, he'll think you're in danger and come barging back from fighting the fires. He'll be in there cleaning house before we know what's going on."

Chelsea almost laughed. "You've got that right."

"Stay where you are and act as if nothing is wrong. After you leave work, come meet me."

"At SinCas?"

"No. How about Angelique's Coffee Shop?"

She had no problem with that, but that seemed like an odd place, especially with so many people around—or maybe that was the point. "Okay. I get off work at five. See you then."

"Good. Stay safe."

Easy for her to say. Chelsea tucked away her phone and worked harder than she ever had before, all the while keeping a keen ear out for Marty or Stick. She didn't know what kind of shifter either of them might be, but chances were that one of them at least, was a dragon. While she'd never fought one, she could only imagine that she'd be the one who ended up dead.

When five o'clock rolled around, she slipped into the front office, punched her card, and hightailed it out of there. The moment her butt hit the car seat and the engine fired up, she let out a big sigh of relief.

Not only was it terrible that Stick might be holding some shifters against their will, Chelsea wasn't sure she could go back to work at the shelter now. Both Marty and Stick scared her. Hopefully, Kaleena would have answers.

Once in town, she parked in back of the coffee shop and entered through the rear entrance. Because Kaleena hadn't arrived yet, Chelsea went ahead and ordered a coffee and a small ham sandwich. Angelique wasn't out front, which might be a good thing. Sharing Chelsea's discovery with a stranger probably wouldn't be smart.

She carried her order number over to a table and sat down, her mind racing. Had she really sensed shifters, or had her hormonal mind played some trick on her? All of the cages had animals in them. That much was a given. It might have been the silver collars that made her think something sinister was going on. If they were merely quarantined, why collar them?

"Chelsea?" Kaleena stood at the table with an order number in her hand. Obviously, Chelsea had been so lost in her own thoughts she hadn't noticed that Kaleena had arrived at least a minute or two ago. As soon as Kaleena slid across from her, Chelsea could feel her muscles relax.

"Tell me exactly what you saw," Kaleena said.

Chelsea inhaled. "Mind you my imagination might have gotten the best of me, but I broke into Stick's office and—"

"Hold it right there. You broke in? He'll figure out that you uncovered his secret then."

"Maybe not. I picked the lock but locked it before I left."

Kaleena's mouth twisted. "If he is keeping illegal contraband back there, he'll have surveillance cameras everywhere. Did you see any?"

Her heart dropped to her stomach. "I, ah, didn't look." Shit.

Kaleena blew out a breath. "Let's hope he isn't that sophisticated. Go on."

Chelsea detailed what she believed she saw, though in the retelling, it sounded implausible. "I should have snapped a picture, but before I could even think, Stick returned."

"He didn't see you leave his office, did he?"

She shook her head. "No. I managed to get out of there and duck into the bathroom before he entered the building, but if he had been paying attention at all, he would have smelled the scent of his animals. When I opened the door, the aroma went everywhere."

"Crap. He might think someone else snuck in if you were in the bathroom."

"It's possible," she said, but Chelsea wasn't optimistic.

"If he didn't run after you right away, we have some time to figure out a plan."

"You said you'd contact some of...you know who." She didn't want to mention the Guardians in a public place.

"Yes. I called my father. He's looking into it."

"He can't just barge in and demand to look in the back, can he? At least on Earth, he'd have to get a warrant. Stick has rights."

She shook her head. "No, but there's nothing illegal about flying over and trying to sense any shifters. If they find concrete evidence, they'll move in."

That sounded okay. "What should I do? I'm almost afraid to go into work tomorrow."

The waitress carried over their drinks and Chelsea's sandwich. The aroma from the steaming brew helped perk her up.

"Call in sick tomorrow until we can figure out what to do."

That made a lot of sense. "I can do that. Does Declan know what happened? Or Finn?"

She shook her head. "Finn's working tonight, so I haven't had a chance to fill him in yet, but once I tell him, he'll want to rush over to the shelter and break into the back. That, I'm afraid, might ruin things for all involved."

That almost made her laugh. "He would do that. And Declan?"

"I didn't want to bother him until we know more. I fear my brother would do even worse damage. When Declan returns tonight, I'll call him and pass on the information you told me along with anything new we may have uncovered by then. In the meantime, go home and rest. We'll figure something out, I promise." Kaleena shook her head. "I am really sorry you ended up at this shelter. I wanted your experience on Tarradon to be a good one."

Chelsea reached across the table and squeezed her hand. "It has been. Everyone has been amazing. Okay, not everyone, but most people have been."

Kaleena smiled. For the rest of their visit, they chatted about Kaleena's job. As much as Chelsea was tempted to broach the topic of being pregnant, she wanted Declan to be the first to hear the news.

"You're going straight home, right?" Kaleena asked.

"Yes, but then I need to go for a run to clear my head." She could see Kaleena about to protest. "It's safer when I'm in my wolf form. Trust me."

"You're right. You can hide easier." She tapped her chest. "I know, remember?"

Chelsea kept forgetting that Kaleena could now shift into wolf form too. Once they finished, they left a tip and headed out. After hearing Kaleena's plan, Chelsea was far less tense than on the drive over. She'd go for a run, and then settle in at home with a good book. If she couldn't have Declan, she could fall in love with some book boyfriend.

True to her word, as soon as she arrived at the cabin, she ditched her clothes, stepped onto her front porch, and shifted. The evening light was growing dim, but her shifter eyes had no problem seeing where to run. After taking these paths for a few weeks, Chelsea had her favorites. Because water was calming to her, she headed toward the stream. Charging down the path, she let the wind blow in her face. Many of the smells reminded her of Declan, which unfortunately made her worry. What if something happened to him while he was battling the fires? Finn had told her that fire wasn't a big threat to a dragon, but that it could do some damage with prolonged exposure.

She sighed, wishing Declan were with her right now. They had so much they needed to discuss. If only he could run with her, life would be complete.

A few feet before she reached the fork that led to the stream, a huge ache charged up her leg. A second later, she tumbled forward. Even though she reached out to stop from losing total control, she still landed on her snout. Shit.

It took a second to register that her leg was caught in something. Chelsea's breaths whooshed out of her as she rolled over to assess the situation. Really? How the hell had she let herself be caught in a trap? Two metal plates pinned her leg tight. And it hurt like a bitch.

Stop struggling, her wolf said. *The skin is already cut.*

Double crap. Just as she debated whether she should shift and pry open the plates with her hands, something stung her neck. She swatted at it with her paw, only to realize she'd been shot with a dart. What the hell?

Her ability to focus vanished, and lifting her paw became impossible.

Wait! Footsteps sounded far away—or at least it appeared as if they were at a distance. A few seconds later, Marty's face loomed over her. Marty did this to her? She opened her mouth, but all that came out was a whine.

Part of her wanted to shift and ask him what was going on, but for starters, she'd be naked, and secondly, with the way her body was growing weak, she wasn't sure she could shift even if she wanted to.

He reached out and stroked her fur. "Stay calm." He plucked out the dart and tossed it away. "We need to get you out of this trap. What kind of asshole puts a trap in the middle of a running trail?"

Her mind fuzzed. Marty hadn't set the trap? Who had then?

Stick? Did it really matter?

Marty pulled apart the spring, and Chelsea clawed the ground to move forward, only her progress was measured in inches instead of feet. As much as she wanted to run away and lick her wounds, nothing seemed to work. Oh, no. She'd been drugged. Her baby!

DECLAN WAS EXHAUSTED. Half of the day had been spent fighting the fires that were destroying the farmers' crops, and the other half was searching for the bastards responsible for the destruction. None of the six Guardians had uncovered anything, which sucked.

"What do you want to do now?" Thane asked. "Stay here tonight or go home and try to get a good night sleep?"

Declan scanned the horizon. "The fires are contained for now."

"But for how long?"

"We can't camp here indefinitely. We'll need some leads."

"How about Griffin and I keep a close eye on things here, and you and the rest of the guys head back. Hopefully, Logan can do some searching on the dark web to get a hint about who might be responsible."

That was a good idea. "Are you thinking they will strike again tonight?" Declan asked. "If so, I'll stay."

"No. I'm suggesting Griff and I stay tonight just as a precaution. We can reconvene tomorrow at SinCas to discuss strategy."

"Sounds good." It didn't matter if he stayed or went. It was too late to see Chelsea anyway since it was already past eleven. Tomorrow, after the group came up with a plan of action as to how to handle these arsonists, he would stop by and see her.

The flight home was wonderfully uneventful, but even in his dragon form, he could smell the smoke in the air and on his scales. A shower was definitely on the agenda. While he wanted to hear Chelsea's voice, it was better if he didn't call. Knowing her, she'd suggest he come over. Given she had to be up early for work tomorrow, it would be best if he let her rest.

Chelsea, Chelsea. It was all he thought about.

Once home, Declan stripped and jumped in the warm shower. He was totally conflicted. With each passing day, his need and desire for her grew. The problem still remained that it wouldn't be fair to her—or to him—if they lived together. He was already falling in love with her and losing her might kill him. One contributing factor to this intense attraction was the fact that she was the first woman who didn't want anything from him. Not his money. Not his protection. And not his time. Bess had been selfless too, but she'd been his mate.

Last week, he'd tried staying away from Chelsea for both of their sakes, and his resolve had lasted all of six days. No, the only solution seemed to be to enjoy Chelsea for as long as he could. If and when her mate showed up, he'd have to let her go—painful as it would be.

He huffed out a laugh. No one said life was fair.

Chapter Fifteen

EXHAUSTED FROM THE day's physical exertion, Declan slept deeply. He would have slept in longer had his cell not rung and awoken him. Naked, he jumped out of bed, rushed to the kitchen and grabbed his cell off the counter. Oh, shit. It was Kaleena. "What's wrong?"

"I've been leaving you messages since last night." Her tense tone caused every protective cell in his body to fire. His mind had been on Chelsea, and he hadn't checked the screen after he jumped in the shower. "Sorry. I got home late. What's up?"

"Don't freak out, but Chelsea thinks she saw something illegal happening at the shelter yesterday."

That didn't sound so bad. While stolen pets were a hardship to the owner, all they had to do was search a few shelters for them. He leaned his elbows on the counter. "What exactly did she see?"

Kaleena described the cages, the collars, and the possible shifter signatures. His mind raced. "I can't help but think the Royals are involved," his sister said.

He jackknifed upright. "Fuck. Is Chelsea at the shelter now?"

"No. She agreed to call in sick today. I spoke with Dad last night, and he's figuring out a plan. We can't just barge in there."

He could. "I'll do a quick check at the shelter right now to see if I spot anything."

"No. We don't want to tip off this guy, Stick."

She had such little faith in him. "I'll pretend I need to speak with Chelsea. Stick will tell me she's home sick, and I'll leave, but not before I try to sense other shifter signatures." Though sensing the identities of multiple ones was next to impossible.

"Okay, but don't be obvious."

"I know what I'm doing."

"You better. We don't want her boss to come after Chelsea."

That was the last thing he wanted too. He disconnected and quickly dressed. The team was regrouping at SinCas to discuss the fires, but he might have to be a little late. He made a quick call to his father to explain his dilemma.

"Definitely check out the shelter, but be careful."

"I also want to talk to Chelsea when I'm finished. Then I'll head on in to the meeting."

"If you miss anything, I'll catch you up," his dad said.

"Thanks."

As soon as he disconnected, Declan flew to the shelter. As he neared the main building, he swooped low enough in order to sense any shifter signatures. Only one registered. That was odd since Chelsea had said she'd noted a few when she'd seen the ten cages.

Declan landed and ambled over and into the building, checking for surveillance cameras. He spotted one in the main lobby. A door opened in the back, and Stick came into view. "Hey, Declan."

The man seemed friendly enough. "I need to talk to Chelsea for a minute. I didn't see her outside. I trust she's here someplace?"

He shook his head. "She called in sick today."

Declan widened his eyes, trying to look surprised. "Did she say what was wrong?"

"No, but I know she hasn't been feeling well for a few days now."

That troubled him. "I'll stop by her place then. Thanks."

Stick smiled. "No problem. Nice to see you again."

He doubted that. "You too."

As soon as Declan stepped outside, he took off, confused about a few things. He didn't like that Chelsea had been ill and had said nothing to him. When he'd stopped over after work the other day, she looked healthy to him. He'd ask her about it for sure.

Even though the cabin was in the woods, his father had trimmed back the trees leading up to the cabin to allow for dragon access. When Declan spotted her car parked in front, he relaxed. After shifting, he jogged up the steps and knocked on her door. "Chelsea, it's me, Declan."

When she didn't answer, his body shot to alert. He called her cell, and it rang inside. What was going on? "Chelsea, open up, please."

Perhaps she was really sick, though it was possible she could be in the shower, still asleep, or wasn't ill and had gone for a run. A quick walk around the cabin convinced him she'd decided to enjoy her day off. Given her car was here, a run seemed the most plausible explanation. He might not be a wolf, but his two legs could transport him quite well.

She'd mentioned a few of her preferred trails. Her favorite was to the waterfall. As a kid, he and his siblings had often gone there. Needing to see her, Declan took off at a trot. Because he wasn't sure if wolves kept to the trails or if they liked to cut through the underbrush, he scoped out the entire area.

He couldn't remember the last time he went jogging, though right now, his body was enjoying the exercise, despite being bone weary after yesterday's trials.

As he neared the fork that led to the waterfall, something caught his eye. Maybe it was the way the sunlight was streaming through the branches or how he'd moved to the side of the path to avoid a dip, but a metal stake stuck up from the ground that shouldn't have been there. Attached to it was a chain. He might have ignored it had the scent of blood not caught his attention.

Hoping there was some innocent reason for it being there, Declan knelt down. A carabiner was attached to the chain, and next to it was a splotch of blood. If by some horrible chance, Chelsea stepped in a trap, all she had to do was shift, pull open the jaws of the trap, and escape. Shifting back into her wolf form would have allowed her to heal quickly. His imagination might have gotten the best of him.

Some other animal might have stepped in the trap.

Just as he was about to continue on, something yellow peaked out from a pile of leaves. He parted them to expose a dart. He wasn't a hunter since the whole idea was abhorrent to him, but if there had been a trap, why sedate the animal?

Declan stood. Hunting wasn't illegal, and as much as he'd like to find this person who shot the dart, Declan had better things to do—like find Chelsea. He took off at a run toward the waterfall, hoping to find her sitting on the side, either drinking from the river or sunning herself. When he arrived though, no one was there.

"Chelsea?" He called her name several times, but only the wind answered.

Declan searched the area thoroughly. Damn. She must have taken a different path. Determined to find her, he returned to the fork and headed down the other branched path. For the next hour, he searched everywhere but came up empty. There were miles of possibilities. Unless he had help, he'd never be able to search them all.

He headed back to the cabin wondering if a friend had stopped by and taken Chelsea to lunch or maybe to a doctor's appointment. If so, she should have returned. However, when he arrived at the cabin, she still wasn't home. Worried, he called Finn at the office.

"Hey, you missed the meeting," Finn said as a way of greeting.

"I had a good reason. I can't find Chelsea, and I'm worried."

"Oh fuck. About two hours ago, I had this pain shoot up my leg, but I dismissed it. Do you think it could be my twin link acting up?" Finn asked, his tone deep and full of concern.

Declan didn't want to consider that Chelsea had been the one in the trap, but he gave Finn a quick rundown. "I then went to the waterfall and ran down a few other paths, but I couldn't find her."

"I can find her. My wolf is excellent at scenting blood—especially if it belongs to my twin. I'll be there as soon as I can."

It was the best he could hope for. "Thanks."

Declan paced, all the while trying to figure out where Chelsea might have gone. Calling in sick and then heading into town could get her canned. No, she was smarter than that. She'd keep a low profile. So, where was she? Was she seeing a doctor? He refused to face the possibility that she had been trapped and tranquilized. There had to be a good explanation.

Stick hadn't acted smug or scared that his secret might have gotten out, nor had he acted as if he was worried that Declan might uncover something. He finally concluded that Stick hadn't harmed Chelsea. Damn. Then who had—assuming she had been harmed?

Finally, after what seemed like forever, Finn arrived.

"Anything?" Finn asked as he rushed over to Declan.

"Nothing. When I called Chelsea, her phone rang inside the cabin, so she wouldn't have contacted anyone."

"Did you look inside for her?" he asked Declan.

"No, but I didn't sense any shifter signature." He stuck a hand in his pants. "I have the key though."

"If she went for a run, she would have stashed the under the mat or something."

He waved the key. "This works too."

Together, they went in. Chelsea's jeans and shirt were tossed on the back of the sofa. "It looks like she went out for a run," Finn said. "She never was the neatest when she left her stuff in the house."

"We've got to go over the trail again."

Finn nodded. "Where did you say you saw that stake?"

The memory of the blood on the stake churned his gut. "Maybe a mile up the path. It's a couple hundred of feet before the path forks."

"I'd suggest we call Birk, Logan, or Thane, but they all left to find the culprits who lit the fires."

"Damn." More guilt assaulted Declan for not lending a hand, but Chelsea had to come first.

"I'll race ahead. If you hear me howl, come fast," Finn said.

"I will. Now, go."

Finn and he raced out of the house. Seconds later, Finn shifted into his wolf form. Declan always thought being a dragon was the best shifter to be in the world. Now he understood why having the ability to shift into more than one animal would give him an added edge. Both his sister and Finn were lucky to possess the ability to choose between two animal forms.

Finn disappeared down the path, and Declan followed. This time, he focused more on his senses. Declan was sure he'd be able to smell her delicious scent or notice if she'd gone off the path. "Chelsea?" he called.

Not that he expected an answer, but if she were injured, he might hear a whimper or a small howl. Before he'd traveled a half-mile, Finn howled, and Declan's heart stopped. He'd found something. Declan sprinted down the path, flying over the rocks, and batting away the branches in his way. When he reached the stake on the side of the path, Finn was in his human form.

"What is it?" Declan asked.

"It's Chelsea's blood."

Declan's muscles almost gave way. "Are you sure?"

"I know my twin's scent."

"If some fucker trapped her, why tranquilize her?"

"Either he wasn't a shifter and didn't know she was one, or he knew damn well it was Chelsea and couldn't afford for her to talk," Finn said.

Fuck. "No wonder her boss had been so calm. He probably ordered her to be captured."

"Are you positive it's him, or are you guessing?" Finn asked.

"I'm guessing."

"Then I say we continue to look for her. Let me call Kaleena. The two of us can search faster."

The man he had saved on Earth, Ronan, had been a tracker—a man with the ability to find anyone by his scent. If all else failed, Declan might have to ask for his help.

Finn pocketed his phone. "Kaleena will be here as fast as she can."

"That's great. I've already checked the area around the waterfall, but maybe I missed something."

"If Chelsea was captured, there's no telling where they took her. It could be in this part of the countryside or far away."

Acid churned in his stomach. "What do you suggest? We can't just sit on our hands," Declan said. "We have to look everywhere."

"Agreed," Finn said. "I think we should have Kaleena travel the paths in her wolf form, while you and I take to the skies."

"If they have Chelsea in a building, how can we find her?" Declan asked. Usually, he was the one with the ideas. Now, his brain had ceased to function.

"I might be able to sense where she is, assuming she's conscious. At least on Earth we could do that."

He inhaled. "We need to try."

They returned to the cabin just as Kaleena was landing. She quickly shifted. "What's the plan?"

Finn filled her in. Once she shifted and sped away, Finn and Declan flew off. For the second time in his life, it was as if he lacked the skills to save the person he was fast falling in love with.

Chapter Sixteen

WHEN CHELSEA OPENED her eyes, the pain in her head defied description. The last thing she remembered was Marty hovering over her, offering his help. Blood was caked on her right front paw where the trap had clamped down on her. That was curious. Why hadn't her wolf healed her yet?

Chelsea rose to all fours, teetered, and dropped back down. Whatever had been in that dart was still messing with her head. Daylight streamed in the window, so she probably hadn't been unconscious for long. The metal cage she was in really pissed her off though. Chelsea debated shifting, but her human form might not fit in the small space. The lock on the outside of the cage would be impossible to pick without something sharp to poke it with.

Only then did she notice the heavy weight around her neck. She lifted a paw and batted at it. Oh shit. While she couldn't see what it was, from the feel, it was a metal collar—just like the ones she'd seen around the necks of the caged shifters in the back room at the shelter.

Her heart nearly stopped at the implication. Not only wouldn't she get out of there, no one would find her either. Hell, she bet no one was aware anything had happened. Declan wouldn't be stopping over until tonight, and even if he worried when she didn't answer her door, he wouldn't be running all over the woods to find her—assuming she was still in the woods. The lack of horns honking and wheels zinging on pavement implied she wasn't in some city warehouse. This seemed to be a house of some sort though.

"Hello, Chelsea."

A growl erupted from her throat. Sabrina! She should have

known. Despite the tight quarters, Chelsea was almost tempted to shift just to give her a piece of her mind.

Sabrina paced around the cage. "Are you wondering why I captured you?"

Chelsea growled deeper, but it took a lot of effort.

"Let me tell you. I'm hoping to lure Kaleena here."

Chelsea dropped back onto her haunches, in part because her strength was weakening. She did manage a small howl however.

"Mind you, your snooping caused you to be caught sooner rather than later. You never should have gone into the back room. Stick was angry, but I was secretly glad. It just moved up my timeline."

She wasn't making any sense. What kind of timeline? Chelsea pawed at her collar—a collar that was probably made of silver if the hot spots on her neck were any indication. Wolves and silver did not mix, but she would do whatever it took to escape. The how was the big question.

Despite the lack of space, she needed to shift. She prayed the collar didn't choke her since her human neck might be larger than her wolf's neck.

Concentrating on changing form, Chelsea tried but failed. Maybe it was the drugs that were preventing her, though she'd never failed at changing form before even when under any kind of influence.

Sabrina laughed. "Don't waste your energy trying to shift. I put a spell on you. You can't shift." With that she walked away.

Who was this person? Declan never mentioned anything about Sabrina having any kind of powers. Guess he was fooled. Damn.

As if someone had taken over her body, her muscles gave way first and then her vision.

AFTER FLYING FOR hours, Declan and Finn were no closer to

locating Chelsea than before. With each flap of his wings, Declan was slowly losing hope. He motioned they return to the cabin to regroup.

"What now?" Finn asked once they landed. "She has to be somewhere."

"I'm going to talk to Stick again. I'm certain he was lying. We should both go. I can talk to him while you look around, though I don't have much hope she's anywhere near the shelter."

"You believe he's involved?" Finn asked.

"It seems highly likely."

"Let me tell Kaleena our plans." He looked off to the side and communicated with his mate telepathically. "She'll keep searching and said to go ahead without her. Let's do this."

A few minutes later, they landed in the shelter parking lot. The animals were all in their pens, but no one was about. He motioned for Finn to check the back while Declan went inside. Just as he stepped in, Stick exited from the hallway. "Declan."

"Chelsea's not home."

"Like I said, she called in sick. Maybe she's in the hospital."

Bullshit. "I found her blood on a trail outside her house."

Stick stabbed a hand through his hair. "Fuck. Marty must have done something to her then."

"Marty?" He was just a flunky, according to Chelsea.

"He's had the hots for her since the moment she came to work here. Marty is a crow shifter. I've seen him fly overhead and follow her. I warned him to stay away from her, but clearly, he didn't listen." Stick looked behind him as if he could sense Finn rumbling around. "Who else is out there?"

"Finn McKinnon, Chelsea's twin brother. He can sense her whereabouts."

"She's not here, I swear. Talk to Marty."

Declan wasn't so sure he believed him, but maybe Marty knew something. "Where does Marty live? Or is he working today?"

"He called in sick too. Convenient don't you think?" Stick gave him directions to Marty's place.

"Thank you." It took all of his control to say those two words.

Declan raced out the door and motioned for Finn to join him. "Anything?" he asked his sister's mate.

"Nothing. No other shifters on the premise either."

"He must have moved them then."

"What did he say about Chelsea?" Finn asked.

"He thinks that his assistant, Marty, might have followed her and done something to her. I have the directions to his house. Let's check it out," Declan said.

"Lead the way."

"I need to stop at the mine for something. It won't take too much time."

"No problem."

From there, it didn't take them long to reach the house. Marty was outside, washing his car. When he spotted them, fear streaked across his eyes. Too bad accusing him outright would only cause Marty to clam up.

They both landed. Declan strode up to him. "Hey, you're Marty, right?"

"Yeah."

"I'm Declan Sinclair, Chelsea's friend."

Finn stepped forward. "And I'm her twin brother."

"Something happen to her?" Marty asked, his gaze shifting from right to left.

"You could say that," Declan said. "We found her blood on the path near her cabin, and we think something bad happened to her." So much for sounding non-threatening.

"Oh, no. I'm sorry to hear that."

"Your boss said you've been following her. We were hoping you saw who might have harmed her."

He glanced down to the ground. "No, I swear. I knew she wasn't feeling well, so I left her alone."

From his poor eye contact, he was lying. Beating the answer out of someone rarely ever worked, but Declan was tempted to try. "If you hear of anything, give me a call." Declan handed him a SinCas card with his number on it.

"Sure thing." His chest caved, as if he'd finally let out a long held breath.

While Declan was chatting with Marty, Finn had slipped a tracking device under the man's bumper. It was why Declan had wanted to stop at the mine.

Since Marty hadn't been helpful, they decided to head back to SinCas and regroup.

"I'll let Kaleena know to meet us there," Finn said.

"Sounds good."

When they arrived, Kaleena had beaten them back. Thane and their dad had returned from fighting the fires, while the rest of the team remained behind. His dad kept saying he was retired, but Declan would never believe him until he stayed home for more than two days.

They met in the conference room. Once they fixed something to drink, the five of them sat down.

"What do we know?" Declan's dad asked.

He filled him in on finding Chelsea's blood along the path. "The trail went cold after that, so we headed over to the shelter. While I kept Chelsea's boss busy, Finn looked around."

"I saw no evidence of discarded cages or shifters held against their will," Finn said.

His father dragged a hand down his chin. "Chelsea's disappearance practically confirms that what she saw was real."

"I agree," Declan said.

"When she called to tell me about what Stick was hiding, she was scared," Kaleena said. "The silver collars around the shifters' necks imply that the Royals are involved."

"Most likely," their dad said. "We'll have to wait for the rest of the Guardians to return before we fly over the castle. I'm not sure what we'll learn though. Any idea what our not-so-friendly relatives are up to? I'll have to say that as long as they have been in power, I've never heard of them incarcerating people in their shifter form."

Kaleena shook her head. "No, but remember what I went through. They do seem fond of sedating a person and then taking away her powers. The more I think about it, the more this smacks of Sanditra, that bitch dark witch who tried to ruin me when I was held captive by our Royal relatives."

Declan didn't care who was responsible. He just wanted Chelsea back. "I know that look in your eye. What are you thinking, Kaleena? I hope you aren't planning on talking with Sanditra."

Kaleena laughed, but it held no joy. "Never. She'd probably steal my powers again. But there is one person who might know where Sanditra is."

"Who?"

"Danita."

"Is that one of the women who Lily had saved from the bowels of the castle—the white lighter?" Finn asked.

"Yes. She was with Sanditra for weeks after I left. Sanditra might have let something slip about stealing shifters or something."

"I'm not so sure Danita can help. Griffin has mentioned her often. In fact, I know he checks up on her. She's never recovered from the trauma."

"Does she have post-traumatic stress disorder or something?" Finn asked.

"Griffin said it's something like that."

"What do you think we should do, Declan?" Kaleena asked.

"I don't know; we can't just sit here though." He picked up the phone and punched in Griffin's number. Most likely, his cousin would be at work right in the building. His job as head of sales was too valuable to have him fight the fires.

"Where are you?" Griffin said.

"In the conference room." He explained about Chelsea being missing.

"What can I do?"

He explained Kaleena's theory. "Listen, we are desperate. We've looked everywhere for her. It really does seem that the Royals might be involved, and that means Sanditra could have had a hand in this. We're thinking Danita might be able to help us."

"No."

His cousin's sharp tone surprised him. The door to the conference room opened, and Griffin marched in with his cell pressed to his ear. He disconnected and then leaned his hands on the table. He glanced from Declan to Finn to Kaleena and then to his uncle. "I know how important Chelsea is to all of you, but there has to be another way. Danita is really fragile right now."

"We aren't asking her to confront her nemesis. We just want to know if Sanditra ever mentioned where she lived or what she liked to do in her spare time—when she wasn't trying to infect people with her darkness," Declan said.

Kaleena huffed out a laugh. "I doubt the bitch would give anything away, but as I said, Danita was with her longer."

Griffin pulled up the chair. "Do you actually think Danita knows how to find Sanditra?"

"No, but she might possess a clue to help us. Can you ask her?"

Griffin looked off, his leg bouncing under the table. The three people who Lily helped set free from the prison cell had been treated, both physically and mentally, but apparently Danita was in the worst shape of them all.

"I'll ask, but I won't push. She's fragile."

Griffin's protectiveness surprised Declan. "Just give it a try."

Griffin pulled out his phone, inhaled, and tapped a button. "Danita, it's me."

He pushed back his chair and walked toward the door as if he needed privacy. What was that about? Declan wasn't even aware the two knew each other that well. Clearly, he needed to touch base with his relatives more often.

Griffin returned to the table. "She was hesitant, but when I explained that the Royals might have captured Chelsea, she said she'd come in, though she doesn't know how she can help."

"That's all we can ask," Declan said.

If Danita couldn't give them a clue, he didn't know where to turn next. The Four Sisters of Fate often gave assistance but only when Fate was involved, and since Chelsea wasn't his mate, he didn't think they could help. Well, damn.

Chapter Seventeen

"LIKE I TOLD Griffin over the phone, I don't know where Sanditra hides out when she's not somewhere torturing her prisoners." Danita's bitterness nearly cut Declan in half.

Kaleena reached out and clasped Danita's hand. "Do you remember where you were when you were taken? I know I was in The Wing's Bar when I was drugged."

"I was in the woods taking a hike. The forest centers me."

"What woods?" Kaleena asked.

"The ones around Sandalwood Lake."

Declan looked at the others. "How did they capture you?" he asked.

Danita worried her fingers, her gaze unfocused. Kaleena ran a gentle hand down her arm. "Danita? Are you okay?"

She looked up. "What? Oh, sorry."

"How did they capture you?" Kaleena asked again.

"I was sitting on a rock, enjoying the forest and its surroundings, when I felt something sting me. The next thing I remember is waking up in a cell."

Declan wasn't sure if he should push her, in part because his usually calm cousin was glaring at him. "Did Sanditra ever mention a place where she likes to practice her dark magic?"

Danita shook her head. "I spent weeks with that bitch, and it nearly killed me. She escorted me somewhere once, but I wasn't conscious at the time. I'm a strong white lighter, but she's something else altogether. So much dark magic and power."

Declan's gut nearly erupted. The thought of Chelsea anywhere near her sickened him.

"What happened at this other place?" he asked, keeping his voice low and soft.

"When I awoke, she infused me with her dark powers, but I kept fighting her off. I sometimes feel as if she still has a hold on me."

"Then what?" he asked.

"She took me back to my cell. I guess I was a hard nut to crack."

"I'm sorry that happened. I take it Sanditra never mentioned anyplace she likes to go then?"

"Sanditra doesn't like anything. When I was at that house though, I smelled lake water."

Declan sat up straighter. "Were you inside or out?"

"Outside."

"What did the house look like?" he asked.

She glanced at Griffin, acting as if he had the answers.

"Go on," Griffin urged.

"It was on the small side. White and wooden." She ran her hands down her face. "I'm sorry. My memory is really bad. For all I know, I never really left my cell. Sanditra can do things to a person's mind to make you think one thing when in reality, something else is happening."

Kaleena nodded. "I know." She looked up at Declan, clearly imploring him to end this discussion.

"Thank you, Danita. You've been helpful."

She lifted her head, and her eyes sparkled for the first time. "I hope you find Chelsea."

"Me too."

Griffin escorted her out of the conference room. "So now what?" Finn asked.

"There aren't a ton of lakes around here. I think it might be time to see The Four Sisters of Fate," Declan said.

"Chelsea is not your mate. Will they help?"

"I'm hoping they will if it is a matter of life or death."

With a promise to let everyone know if he learned anything,

Declan took off for the Four Sisters Pottery shop. Usually, the Guardians went at night when customers wouldn't be around, but time was critical. If Sanditra had Chelsea, how long could a non-white lighter hold out?

When the shop came into view, he landed. Two cars were parked in front. Damn. He shifted and entered, careful not to knock over any of the beautiful pots or other trinkets. Magnolia was with two women, so he pretended to look around, but he was so jittery, he worried he might chase the two customers away. Someone touched his arm, and he jumped. He spun around. "Acacia."

"Hey, Declan. You seem agitated."

What gave it away—the fisting of his hands, the pacing, or the clenched jaw? "I am. Finn's sister is missing. I think Sanditra might have her."

Her eyes narrowed. "Sanditra? Come into the back where we will have privacy."

Thankfully, she seemed willing to at least listen, he followed her. Once in the back, they sat at the four-person table that was lightly dusted with dry clay.

"Tell me what's happened." For the next few minutes, he regaled her with what they had learned. "You believe Sanditra is involved because Chelsea saw these silver cuffs—the same kind the Royals used on the white lighters, right?" Acacia asked.

When she said it that way, the evidence seemed thin. "Yes. Honestly, I don't care who has her. I just want her back. I need to find her."

Acacia leaned back in the seat, her gaze scanning the room. She sat back up and faced him, her lips pressed together. "Okay. I'll help, but I'll need something of hers—like a hairbrush."

"Are you going to extract DNA or something?" Declan didn't think that was how these sisters worked. Magic was more their style.

"Not quite, but the hairbrush will contain her life force."

That made more sense. "I'll get it and be right back."

Declan rushed out of the store, thankful he didn't knock anything over. Keeping low to the ground for maximum speed, he raced to her cabin in the woods.

Once there, he entered the house, trying not to picture all of the places where they'd made love. It was hard enough to keep his imagination in check, mostly because her scent was everywhere. Why was he so drawn to her when she wasn't his mate? Now wasn't the time to figure that out though. First things first: find Chelsea, and then try to discover why he wanted to be with her so much.

Her hairbrush was in a drawer in the bathroom. He looked around to see if there was anything else he should take, but nothing stuck out. Declan ran out of the house, locked the door, and took off.

By the time he arrived back at the pottery shop, Declan was almost out of breath from flying so fast. As soon as he landed, he shifted and rushed inside. Inhaling to calm down, he strode to the back. Magnolia, Acacia, and Poppy were there waiting for him. He didn't see their fourth sister, Primrose, but she was probably nearby.

"Declan, I'm sorry to hear about Finn's sister," Magnolia said.

"Thank you."

She ran a gaze up and down his body. "She means a lot to you, doesn't she?"

Did that mean they were mates? "Yes."

"Then we'll do our best. Have a seat while Acacia, Poppy, and I make a scale for you."

"A scale? What will that do?"

"You'll see." After Magnolia located a small bowl, she gathered some hairs from the brush and ground them up. Acacia added what looked like herbs, and then Poppy said a chant in a strange tongue. With their backs to him, he wasn't able to see what they were doing exactly, but Declan remained quiet, not wanting to break their concentration.

When Magnolia spun around, she held up a clear scale. "Let's take this outside." He recalled they had made something like it for Birk when he'd wanted to be able to sense his mate, Lily.

Acacia handed him back Chelsea's hairbrush, and he stuffed the handle in his shirt pocket, the brush head sticking out.

Once outside, Magnolia asked him to shift. "I'm going to wedge this scale in over your heart. If you draw near to Chelsea, the scale will heat and pulse white."

That sounded good, but there was one flaw. "How close do I need to be to her before it works? I don't know where she is, and the realm is large."

"Honestly, I don't know how close you need to be."

He worked hard not to show his disappointment. These four sisters had been amazing in the past, and he hoped Magnolia was merely being humble. "I appreciate you trying."

Declan shifted and then leaned over to allow Magnolia to place the scale where it needed to go. When she put her palm over his heart, heat singed him.

"This will keep the scale in place—forever. I hope you find her."

So did he. Knowing that time was critical, he took flight for Sandalwood Lake on the off chance Sanditra was holding Chelsea captive there. He could only hope Danita's intel was correct.

Keeping low to the ground, Declan kept his sharp eyes peeled for a house that matched the description Danita had given them. Because the dense foliage blocked a lot of his view, he had to make a pass around the lake twice. As he was about to give up on finding Chelsea today, something white peeked through the trees. The scale on his chest wasn't pulsing or heating, so maybe this would be a wild goose chase. Nonetheless, he needed to check it out. Given its location, he had to go on foot.

After finding the most open space, he landed and then shifted. That speck of white he'd seen from above was now hidden somewhere in front of him. A house implied there'd be a road, so that was where he headed.

Once on the road, Declan took off at a run, searching for Chelsea. He'd seen several homes on the lake, but he doubted Sanditra would be so bold as to hold someone captive where others might notice.

He was halfway around the lake when his scale flickered. Holy shit. This was the right place. Declan stilled, not wanting to give away his presence. As quiet as he could, he continued down the road. Heat seared him, and he slowed. Through the trees, a white house appeared.

Thank you, Acacia, Magnolia, and Poppy.

If he could have remained in his dragon form, he would have cloaked himself. As he neared, he darted tree to tree, stopping at random intervals to avoid being heard. When he came within a hundred feet of the house, he spotted a wolf tied up outside with a silver collar around its neck. Between Finn's description and the fact his scale was bright white, this had to be Chelsea. It took all of his control not to charge toward her.

As much as he wanted to call out, he didn't dare. First, he had to figure out how he was going to free her without the dark witch stopping him. Whether she was inside right now was anyone's guess.

After a bit of thought, he decided to run in, grab Chelsea, and hightail it out of there. If Sanditra was inside, and she tried to stop him, he'd shift and fight her on the ground. He'd never heard of a dark witch being able to withstand flames.

"Chelsea," he whispered.

The animal didn't even lift its head. Either his scale was faulty, or someone was drugging her. The collar might be making her weak too. Declan inhaled and sped toward her. Just as he reached Chelsea, he bent down to untie the rope from around her neck, when the front door opened.

"Well, well, it took you long enough, Declan."

That voice! It sounded so familiar, but the woman saying the words was foreign to him. He stood, unsure of how she knew him. "Sanditra, I assume?"

She smiled. "You assume right. How clever of you." Her tone dripped of sarcasm.

He stood and faced her. "Seems you have something of mine."

Technically, Chelsea didn't belong to him, but it wasn't as if he didn't want to forge a bond with her.

"Is that so? What do I have?"

He didn't buy her innocent act. "This wolf is really a shifter."

She made a grand gesture of covering her mouth. "I had no idea."

Declan didn't need to put up with her bullshit, dark lighter or not. "I'm assuming the collar is preventing Chelsea from shifting. Remove it now! If you don't, I will make your life a living hell because I'm not leaving here without her."

Sanditra rolled her eyes and crossed her arms. "I will if you hand over Kaleena."

The concept was so preposterous, the blood nearly drained from his brain. "Over my dead body."

She smiled. "That can be arranged."

Declan had enough. He lifted his arms and transformed them into claws. Just as he was about to shoot fire at her, an ache raced through him so fast that his muscles caught on fire. He couldn't move. What the hell?

"Goodnight, Declan."

His vision blurred and then turned black. Blind, his muscles gave way, and he collapsed.

Chapter Eighteen

WHEN DECLAN CAME to, it was dawn, and Chelsea wasn't anywhere around. Neither was Sanditra for that matter. Fuck.

How the hell had she been able to paralyze him? He hadn't been shot with a dart. She must have put a spell on him. Crap. His admiration for his sister grew. How had she managed to survive someone as powerful as Sanditra and for such a long time? As for Danita, she was truly amazing.

Needing to find Chelsea, he rose and then staggered. Lowering his hands to his knees, he dropped his head, trying to clear it. That bitch would pay if it was the last thing he did. One thing was certain, he needed more help to find Chelsea. When he did, he would take down that dark lighter.

Because his scale wasn't pulsing, he assumed Chelsea wasn't nearby any longer, but he checked around back just in case. He even tested the front door, but it was locked. The interior was dark, implying no one was there. Where were they? He wouldn't figure it out by standing around and feeling sorry for himself that was for sure.

Moving as quickly as he could, Declan shot down the long driveway. As soon as he found a clearing, he took off and headed straight for SinCas. He could only hope a few of the Guardians were around to help.

During the trip back, he monitored his scale to see if perhaps he could find Chelsea, but unfortunately, it never flashed. On top of the building, he landed harder than usual. His muscles were still not working right.

After a quick check of a few offices, he realized it was too early for anyone to be at work. Needing guidance, he called his dad and explained the situation.

"She paralyzed you?" His dad's tone was a cross between disgust and disbelief that his son couldn't stop her.

"Yes. I hadn't realized how powerful Sanditra is."

"I'll gather the troops. Where are you?"

"At the office."

"Hold tight," his dad said right before hanging up.

Within an hour, many of the Guardians had shown up. Perhaps the most important one was his sister Kaleena. She of all people would understand the dark lighter the best. Along with Kaleena came Finn, Thane, Stone, Tory, Griffin, Nessa, and Declan's dad. The others were either needed at the mine or were battling the fires on the edge of the province.

If this group couldn't find Chelsea and take down Sanditra, no one could. Once they were all seated, he, Kaleena, and Finn brought the others up to speed.

"What's your plan?" his dad asked.

Declan huffed out a laugh. "I don't have one. Thanks to Danita, I found Chelsea, but now that Sanditra knows we're trying to locate her, she'll be more careful."

"I could draw her out," Kaleena said. "She wants me."

"No!" Finn, Declan, and three others shouted in unison.

Finn placed a hand on Kaleena's arm. "We are not exchanging one hostage for another. You know what happened the last time."

"Yes, but you all will be there."

Declan shook his head. "If anything happened to you, I'm convinced Finn would kill me, even if we get Chelsea back."

Kaleena snapped her fingers and then smiled. "I have just the answer."

The room silenced. "What?" Declan asked.

"Who's up for some morning coffee?"

"What the fuck? Chelsea is being drugged and taken somewhere and you want to drink coffee? We have plenty here."

"Do you trust me?"

His sister was acting crazy. "You know I do."

"In order not to overwhelm the coffee shop, how about if only you, Finn, and I go to Angelique's place?"

Tory shook her head. "You are not leaving me out of this. I want to help too. You are my twin, and someone has to make sure you don't sacrifice yourself."

"Fine," Kaleena said, waving a hand and then smiling.

"I could use a strong cup right now," Declan said, "but how will our going there accomplish anything?"

"Angelique is our ace in the hole."

Declan pushed back his chair. "Fine. We'll report back—hopefully, with a plan."

Because it wasn't that far they hopped in Tory's car and headed over. Kaleena was holding something back, but he figured she'd tell them when the time was right.

The shop was about half full when they arrived. Most of the clients were sitting at the counter drinking coffee and snacking on pastries or croissants.

"That's Angelique," Kaleena told Declan.

"I've seen her before. I take it she's a good friend."

"Yes. She's also a very powerful white lighter."

They grabbed a booth near the back. "More powerful than Sanditra?" Declan doubted that.

"I hope so."

Tory slipped out of the booth. "I'll order four coffees."

They told her their preferences.

Declan was sitting across from his sister and Finn. "How do you know Angelique?" he asked Kaleena.

"I came in here for some coffee one day, and the moment I spotted Angelique, I recognized her strength. From there, we've become friends."

He figured there was more to it, but perhaps she didn't want to discuss it in the restaurant. Tory ordered their coffees and then spoke to the owner. Angelique followed Tory back to the booth. She pulled up a chair and sat at the end. "Chelsea is missing?" Angelique said, worry coloring her tone.

"Yes." Once more, Declan gave a brief rundown of what happened.

She shook her head. "That's horrible. Chelsea was in here recently. I recognized her from when Kaleena and she stopped by. Something at work had upset her."

"Did she say what?"

Angelique hesitated. "Apparently your ex-girlfriend stopped by and was a bit snippy with Chelsea."

Fuck. "Sabrina is like that, but she has nothing to do with this. I don't suppose you've met her."

"No, and I'm glad I haven't."

Kaleena reached out and placed a hand on Angelique's. "Is there anything you can do to help?"

"I haven't been here long, but I do have a few contacts who might know something." She pushed back her chair. "Give me a few hours. I'll let you know if I find out anything."

As soon as she left, Declan studied Tory, Kaleena, and Finn. "Do you believe her?" he asked his sister.

"Yes, but even if I didn't, it's not like we have a lot of options," Kaleena said.

Very true. A waitress carried over a tray of coffees and set them on the table. Tory held up her drink. "Here's to finding Chelsea."

"Here, here," they all said in unison.

After they finished their coffees, they headed back to SinCas. He couldn't help but wonder who Angelique would be talking to. Was there a secret group of white lighters that he knew nothing about? If so, why didn't Kaleena know about them?

Hell, even if there were such a group, would they have knowledge of Sanditra's whereabouts?

"Now what?" Finn asked as Tory pulled onto the road.

"We wait to hear what Angelique finds out," Kaleena said. "You guys get back to work while I wait at SinCas. I don't want to be too far away if she contacts me."

"I'll stay too. There's nothing urgent at the mine for me," Declan said.

"Me neither," Finn chimed in.

"I appreciate it."

Kaleena reached across the seat and cupped Declan's shoulder. "Don't worry. We'll find her."

"Let's hope. You saw what Sanditra did to Danita. And she has powers to fend off the dark lighter. I can't imagine what Sanditra will do to Chelsea."

"I want to find her as much as you do," Finn said, "but if Kaleena trusts Angelique, I do too."

Declan nodded. "I'll give her two hours. Then I'm going back out to look for Chelsea."

Keeping her eyes on the road, Tory snapped her fingers. "Maybe we can ask Delisa Contreau to help."

"Who's that?" Finn asked.

"She was the one who was able to connect with Kaleena through me when Kaleena was in the castle cell. Because our twin link was strong, Delisa could hear what was being said and what the place smelled like. She also could feel Kaleena's pain."

"It can't hurt to try."

Declan dragged a hand down his jaw, the acid burning a hole in his gut. "We know that Sanditra has her. I imagine Chelsea will be in some pain if the collar contains poison. I don't know what else she can tell us. I say we wait for Angelique to contact us and then call Delisa as a backup."

"Sounds good," Tory said, though she sounded disappointed.

His sister parked, and everyone entered the SinCas building. On his way up to the top floor, he called his dad and filled him in.

"What do you know about this Angelique woman?"

"Just that she's Kaleena's friend—and a powerful white lighter."

"Are we certain she's not in cahoots with Sanditra?"

His father was talking nonsense. "We would have sensed her darkness—or at least, Kaleena would have. I'll wait to learn what she has to say first before I do anything. Don't worry, I'll take a lot of backup this time if I head out."

"Let me know," his dad said.

"Will do."

Declan tried not to be impatient while waiting two hours, but he failed. He found Finn in Kaleena's office. "Maybe we should go back to the coffee shop and wait there. It'll save time if Angelique learns something."

"What about me and Tory?" Kaleena asked.

"You can't come with us during the search, and Tory would be valuable to Sanditra too."

"I never get to have any fun." His sister shot him a pout, but the worry lines around her eyes had decreased.

Finn slapped his thighs and stood. "The two of us it is."

As they headed out the front door to go to the coffee shop, Angelique was walking toward them. "Angelique. How did you know where to find us?" Declan asked.

"I have many talents."

"What did you find out?" Declan asked.

"I know where Chelsea is. How about gathering the troops and we can discuss the plan?"

"Where is she?" Declan demanded.

She squared her shoulders and faced him. "Plan first."

Arguing would only waste time. He held up his palms in surrender. "Let's go upstairs."

Chapter Nineteen

THE PLAN SEEMED simple enough. Declan, Finn, and Angelique would fly to a house that Angelique claimed held Chelsea—a different one from before.

As soon as they told Thane what was going on, he insisted on helping, claiming he wanted to add his fighting prowess to the already powerful duo of Declan and Finn. Declan suspected his younger brother wanted to go because he found Angelique highly alluring.

Declan pushed back from the conference table. "Everyone ready to free Chelsea?"

"Let's get her," Angelique said with a smile. She really did seem to want to foil Sanditra.

All four of them climbed the steps to the SinCas rooftop. Thane had volunteered to carry Angelique. Thankfully, she didn't balk at his method of transportation.

"We'll lead," she said to Finn and him. "I know where this place is."

That worked for him. "Let's go."

The three of them shifted. Thane picked up Angelique and took off. In the hopes that Declan's scale would flash, they flew close to the ground. Sure enough, when they neared a clearing, heat pulsed over his heart.

A second later, Declan dove toward the ground, and Thane and Finn followed. Once they changed into their human form, they headed in on foot.

Angelique held out her hand to stop them. "Declan, you and

Finn go in first. Thane and I will follow behind."

"Sounds good." Because it was possible that Sanditra would paralyze him again, he motioned for Finn to go around back. Whether Finn could sneak up on her was anyone's guess.

No animal was outside the cabin, but because his scale was flashing white, Chelsea had to be near. They had already discussed tactics. Both he and Thane thought the best approach was for Declan to go in first.

Excitement at seeing Chelsea again mixed with dread. As he stepped up to the front, the door opened.

Sabrina stepped out. "Hello again, Declan."

What the fuck was Sabrina doing there? "Where's Sanditra?"

She laughed. "I really had you fooled, didn't I?"

One moment she was Sabrina and the next she'd transformed into Sanditra. Her change shocked him, but the heated scale on his chest kept him focused. As much as he wanted to ask a hundred questions, he didn't need to become sidetracked. "I want Chelsea."

"Did you bring Kaleena?" she asked with that smug tone of hers.

"No."

Sabrina, or rather Sanditra, crossed her arms over her chest. "No Kaleena, no Chelsea. I thought I made that clear."

"You did." As he moved forward, Sanditra held up an arm, but nothing happened to him. No paralysis. No blindness. No weakening of the limbs.

"What the fuck?" she said. Sanditra's eyes widened, and her mouth gaped open.

"Hello, Sanditra," Angelique said, walking out from behind a tree. Her smile was enough to scare anyone.

"You!"

Declan hadn't even been aware the two of them knew each other. "We've come for Chelsea," Angelique announced.

"You…you can't have her."

Angelique kept her arm extended. Was that her way of keeping the dark lighter at bay? "Who's going to stop us? Surely, you don't believe you can."

Declan's muscles froze, unable to understand the dynamic that was taking place. Angelique was a white lighter like Kaleena, but he'd believed that Sanditra possessed a lot more power.

"Declan," Angelique said. "Get Chelsea. She's inside."

Having no idea how long Angelique could hold Sanditra at bay, he darted around the dark lighter and into the house. The main area consisted of a living room and dining room with a kitchen off to the side.

"Chelsea?" he called out but received no answer.

If his chest scale hadn't been pulsing hot white, he might have believed she wasn't there. The cabin only contained two bedrooms, so it didn't take long before he found her curled up on the floor next to a bed. Declan's pulse soared as he dropped down next to her. "Chelsea? It's me, Declan. Can you hear me?"

Her wolf huffed once but then remained still, her breathing rough and irregular. Damn.

"I'm going to get you out of here. You're going to be okay, I promise." Declan used his calmest tone, mostly to keep from panicking.

He gently scooped her up and carried her outside. Finn, Thane, and Angelique were facing Sanditra, who appeared quite shell-shocked but unfortunately didn't appear defeated.

"You've all made a big mistake," Sanditra said rather smugly to the group as she eyed Chelsea.

Declan must have faltered because Finn scooped Chelsea from his arms. The dark lighter wasn't going to let her go easily. That much was clear. Declan needed to deal with her once and for all. "Finn, take Chelsea away from here."

"You got it."

"Thane and Angelique go with Finn. I don't want anything to happen to her."

Angelique touched his arm. "I'm not leaving."

His younger brother and consummate fighter puffed out his

chest. "Neither am I."

Before he could argue with them, Sanditra transformed into a black dragon laced with lead-colored scales. Holy shit. His senses reeled. How had he not been able to tell that she was a shifter, let alone a dragon shifter? Then again, Nessa and Kyle had run into someone who could mask his dragon signature too. He'd definitely underestimated Sanditra.

She flapped her wings, clearly challenging him to a fight. If he didn't know she was so evil, he'd have almost admired her beauty.

"I want her for myself," he told Thane.

His younger brother held up both hands. "Be my guest. I got your back though."

Declan shifted, and every cell of his being was ready to fight. Now that Chelsea was safe, he could focus on putting an end to this evil woman's life. Drawing on all of his training, Declan charged upward, whipping his tail around, hoping to lasso her hands.

Sanditra must have anticipated his move because she easily dipped out of the way the moment his tail neared. He wasn't discouraged though, because he'd learned over the years that dragon battles were never quick. He would tire her out and then kill her.

Just as Declan was about to try a different approach, she zoomed toward him at a speed he'd never witnessed. Before he could move out of the way, her talons dug into his chest. Pain sliced through him, rendering him unable to move. Dying however wasn't an option. Not only was he a Guardian, Chelsea needed him.

Fighting through the pain, Declan reached up and pierced her neck with his sharp claws. She yelped and released him. While Sanditra didn't seem to be seriously injured, she pulled back, probably toying with him.

We'll toy with her, his dragon said.

Ignoring the pain from the near miss, Declan soared straight up, daring her to follow. Tail whipping behind him and claws extended, he waited until he was high enough before turning around. His plan was to speed downward, hoping his momentum would be so intense that he'd knock her to the ground.

When he finally pivoted, Sanditra was right behind him. How was that possible? He hadn't even sensed her. She breathed fire in his face and then dragged her nails down his wing, nearly ripping it in two. Declan flapped harder and harder, but his injured wing couldn't help keep him aloft for long. Needing to repair, he headed back to the ground.

As if time stood still for him, Sanditra miraculously appeared below him, her talons pointed straight for his chest. Just as she reached out to rip out his heart, Thane swooped in and knocked her out of the way.

Thank you, brother. Normally, Declan fought his own battles, especially when that someone was trying to harm the woman he'd come to love, but with his damaged wing, he might not be able to defeat Sanditra by himself. She had the advantage of some kind of very dark magic.

As much as he needed to rest from the puncture to his chest, he couldn't have the witch harm Thane. Declan rose once more, albeit slowly. Each wing flap caused a tremendous amount of pain, but he needed to reach his brother in order to help.

Just as he was closing in on those two, Sanditra suddenly disappeared. Shit. Declan couldn't locate her. Guardians could always sense another cloaked dragon.

Apparently, not this time.

Thane screeched, his claws scratching the air at some invisible being. Fuck. How could they fight something that was invisible? His own vision blurred, his strength waned, and something akin to acid raced through his veins, rendering his muscles almost useless.

Declan was falling, unable to stop his descent.

Thane sent out a stream of fire just as three gaping holes appeared in one of his wings. Declan flapped to slow his journey to the ground. There had to be something he could do to do help, only what?

Sanditra became visible again and clawed at Thane's snout. It was almost as if she wanted Declan to see her kill his brother. That wasn't going to happen, even if it took his last breath to save him.

Declan roared and drew on all of his strength—strength that was draining fast. He flapped his wings harder, wanting to reach Thane, but all he managed to do was hover in place. Panic filled him at the hopeless situation. When he pictured Chelsea, a bit of joy cut the intensity of the ache. He wouldn't give up. He couldn't.

How ironic that he was a healer, and yet he didn't have the ability to save himself.

Come on, he urged his dragon. *Give me a little more juice.*

I'm trying his animal grunted.

Without warning, something warm and comforting filled him, causing his entire body to glow white. What the hell was going on? Not that he minded because whatever it was helped his wing to heal and his strength to return.

Thank you! You have surpassed anything you've ever done, he said to his dragon.

It wasn't me.

"It was me. Angelique," said a voice inside his head. *"I'm using your body to take that bitch down. We must join forces in order to defeat Sanditra. My white lighter abilities, along with your superior skills, can kill her. Let me do this. Please."*

"Save Thane! That's all I ask."

More heat shot through him, and with it came a strength he'd never experienced before. *"I plan to."*

Declan might have been the one to flap his wings, but it was as if Angelique had taken over his brain, deciding where to go, and how fast to fly. They dove downward, and then quickly shot upward underneath Sanditra. As they neared, his body cloaked.

The black and lead-colored dragon let go of Thane and turned toward them, ready to take them on. His brother only had one fully functioning wing, but he must have sensed something was happening, because he moved out of the way and hovered close by. He'd probably return to the fray if Declan needed him.

As Declan approached his prey, he extended his claws, ready to rip out her dark heart. No longer would Sanditra steal anyone else's powers ever again. This was for Chelsea, Thane, Kaleena, and Danita.

A force inside him festered, and his concentration sharpened.

Destroy the evil! shouted the voice from within. He couldn't tell if it was a command from Angelique, or if his own dragon wanted this victory.

Setting his sights on Sanditra's underbelly, he soared higher and stabbed his talons near to where he thought her heart might be— assuming she even had one. She screeched. A second later, her wings folded in on themselves, and her claws retracted.

Sanditra fluttered her wings and whipped her tail back and forth, but her life force was leaving her. While she gave a valiant effort to stay and fight, she was losing the battle. Declan followed her down to the ground where her dragon collapsed and heaved a final sigh. Right before his eyes, she turned to black dust, and then a gust of wind helped scatter her.

As if someone had ripped the strength from his body, Angelique appeared before him. "I'm sorry I interfered."

Only then did he remember seeing her collapsed on the ground a moment ago. What just happened made no sense, but he was beyond thankful that it had.

"No, I'm happy you did. Thane might have died, and I might have too."

Thane landed with a thud and then collapse. Thane waited for his brother to shift back, but he didn't. His dragon must be trying to heal him. Declan rushed over to his brother and placed a hand on his bleeding chest. Now that Angelique had given him back his strength, he could send all of his healing abilities into Thane.

Angelique knelt down beside him and placed a hand on Thane's snout. "His breathing seems good."

"Yes, but that doesn't mean he'll fly out of here."

He waited for her to explain what the hell had just happened, but she seemed content to stroke Thane's face. Clearly, this woman was a highly powerful white lighter. Since she was able to inhabit his body with such ease, she might be more than an ordinary being. He doubted even the Four Sisters of Fate could have pulled off that trick.

"Why don't you head on back to Chelsea?" Angelique said. "I'll stay here and make sure Thane is feeling better."

From her confident tone, she believed she would have him up and flying in no time. That worked for him. Normally, he would never consider leaving his brother, but he had the sense Angelique was about to perform another miracle and didn't want him to watch.

Declan stood. "I can't thank you enough for—"

Angelique smiled and held up a hand. "No need to thank me."

She leaned closer to Thane as if to protect him.

"Okay."

Angelique pulled out her cell and waved it. "I'll call if I need help."

That provided him with some reassurance. "Thank you."

"Go." She waved an impatient hand.

A bit reluctant, Declan shifted and took off, excited at having Chelsea in his arms again soon.

Chapter Twenty

"**C**HELS?"

Finn was calling to her. Why was he here? She needed to warn him to leave before Sanditra found him, only she couldn't form the words. Sheesh. That was because she was still in her wolf form. Chelsea attempted to shift, but nothing happened. What the hell?

More voices came at her, but she couldn't understand them. While she thought her eyes were open, she couldn't see anything. Her sense of smell seemed to be working though, but not much of anything else. The area smelled of clay. Dry clay. And some sweet scent she couldn't identify. Why couldn't she wake up?

Arms slid under her body. One minute she was inside somewhere and the next she was outside. The fresh air helped perk her up, but it wasn't enough to completely rouse her. Then wind whipped through her fur, and something strong held her close.

When she roused again, the cool wind was gone, but she still wasn't able to open her eyes or shift. Anger and frustration bit into her.

"Chelsea. It's Declan. Can you hear me?"

She wanted to shout for joy. The last time she'd heard his voice, she thought she'd dreamt it. As hard as she tried to move a paw or wag her tail, nothing moved.

DECLAN WAS BESIDE himself. Acacia and Poppy had removed the silver collar from around Chelsea's neck. It was the same kind that

Kaleena had worn when she'd been imprisoned in the castle jail. Finn said that Kaleena felt immediately better afterward, so why wasn't Chelsea responding?

Once the sisters had done all they could for Chelsea, Declan flew her back to the safe house where he planned to stay with her day and night until she was healed. Chelsea hadn't been in battle like his mate had been, but it was just as important to him that Chelsea survive—maybe more so. Even though she didn't appear to have any wounds on her body, she wasn't waking up, and he needed to change that.

Declan placed one hand on her shoulder and the other on her leg, trying to assess the situation. Each injury required its own special treatment. Before he could get a reading on her, a knock sounded on the safe house door.

"Come in," he called.

Finn, Thane, and Kaleena barged in. Kaleena rushed over to them. "How is she?"

He shook his head. "She isn't responding."

Thane placed a hand on Declan's shoulder. "I didn't get to thank you for helping me," his brother said.

"You saved me first." Declan studied him. "I can't believe you healed so quickly. Have you tried to shift?"

"I flew here. My wing is as good as new."

"There were three large holes in your wing. I truly thought you might be permanently damaged."

Thane grinned. "I'm a tough old bird. You should know that."

"How's Angelique?"

Thane's brows pinched. "I have no idea. I thought she was with you."

His pulse soared. "No. She wanted to stay with you until your dragon healed you."

"When I roused, she wasn't there."

Even though Angelique seemed perfectly capable of taking care of herself, he wondered how she'd made it home. If she was able to materialize inside his body, she probably could teleport. Or was she a dragon herself? Before he solved that mystery, he had to heal Chelsea.

Declan ran his hands over her flank and then stilled. Something wasn't right.

"What is it?" Kaleena asked, full of concern.

"I'm feeling another life force."

"Life force, as in an evil part of Sanditra is still inside my sister?" Finn asked as he stepped closer.

Declan's hand trembled. "I can't be sure, but I think she might be pregnant!" His heart jackknifed at the ramification. He glanced from Kaleena to Finn. "Did Chelsea say anything to you two?"

"No," they said in unison.

Declan's healing magic could harm the baby—assuming that was what he was feeling. "I'm not sure what to do."

"Call Greer," Kaleena said.

He wasn't sure how she could help, but the last time he decided not to ask his cousin, Bess had died. He pulled out his phone and contacted her. He gave a shortened version of what went down and that they were at the safe house. "Can you come over?"

"I'm already out the door."

True to her word, Greer showed up ten minutes later. Having so many people in the room was a bit unsettling as it took concentration to heal her. "How about the rest of you grab a bite to eat in the kitchen or something?"

Kaleena rubbed his shoulder. "Sure. We'll get out of your hair, but we won't be far."

"I appreciate that."

Once he and Greer were alone with Chelsea, Declan closed his eyes and placed his hands on her stomach, needing to be sure he had felt a life inside her. "If she is pregnant, I fear my infusive magic might harm the baby."

"May I try?" Greer asked.

"Please. I swear I feel something alive."

"Does that make you happy?" his cousin asked.

"Yes." Declan didn't even hesitate.

Greer placed her hands where Declan's had been. "This is not my forte. I honestly can't tell if she is with child or not."

Another knock sounded on the bedroom door and he sagged, not needing the interruption. "Come in," he called.

To his surprise, Angelique walked in. "How is she?"

"Unresponsive. Did Kaleena call you?"

"No. May I?" she asked.

He had a lot of questions to ask her, but he needed her help more. Not one to turn down her offer, he scooted over. Without actually touching her, Angelique hovered her hands over Chelsea's abdomen. "I'm sensing something."

The confirmation cheered him. "I did too. I think she might be pregnant."

Angelique smiled. "Yes, that must be it. The baby must be protected at all cost."

"I agree, but how?"

"I'll place a sac around the embryo. Any magic—good or bad—won't affect the child."

That was too good to be true. While the Four Sisters might have been able to perform something this amazing, they probably wouldn't have since Chelsea wasn't his mate.

"Would you excuse us for a moment? I want to be alone with Chelsea," Angelique said.

If she hadn't saved his and Thane's life, Declan would have balked. "Sure. We'll wait outside."

If she had a hand in healing Thane, perhaps she'd do the same with Chelsea.

Both he and Greer stepped into the hallway. "Do you trust her?" Greer asked.

"I do. She saved my life and Thane's."

For the next few minutes, he briefly explained how Angelique had basically invaded his body, healed his very serious injuries, and taken over control of his body.

"That sounds like she's some kind of goddess."

He shrugged. "Maybe she is."

The door opened and Angelique motioned them in. Declan tried not to show his disappointment when Chelsea appeared to be the same. "How is she?" he asked.

"She just needs your healing touch. The baby will be fine now. It can't be harmed by any spells or magic you throw at her."

Without thinking, Declan threw his arms around Angelique. "I can't thank you enough."

Embarrassed by his show of emotion, he stepped back and swiped the back of his hand across his eye.

"My pleasure." She said her goodbyes and left as quietly as she came.

For the next few minutes, Declan and Greer poured their healing touch into Chelsea. He'd hoped she'd have awoken by now, but Sanditra must have put one hell of a spell on her. The last time he'd seen anything like this was when Ophelia had called him to Earth to help a friend of Chelsea's. It had taken the two of them to erase that curse. He could only hope that Sanditra wasn't as powerful as that goddess.

AS IF SOMEONE lifted a veil from her brain, Chelsea roused, but she was unsure where she was. Her memory couldn't fill in the blanks.

"Chelsea?"

Wait a minute. That was Declan's voice. That had to mean she had to be safe—or else she'd been dreaming.

"Come on, Chelsea, open your eyes."

She managed a small smile, or at least it felt as if the corners of her mouth lifted. With great effort, she opened her eyes and sighed. Oh, my. What a beautiful sight. Declan was leaning over her, his piercing eyes boring into hers. She wasn't a fan of the wild scruff on his face though. It looked as if he hadn't slept in forever.

Chelsea lifted her arm to wipe away the film from her eyes, only to realize it was a paw. Oh, my goodness, she hadn't shifted. Concentrating, she focused on changing back into her human form.

Declan leaned back as she spun. A second later, she was fully human. Instantly, she wrinkled her nose at the stench. Not only did she smell, her mouth was completely dry. "Water?" she asked as she licked her lips.

As if he were a magician, a glass appeared that he lifted to her mouth. He held up her head as he kept the glass steady. She drank down a few mouthfuls.

"Welcome back," he said with a smile. Declan then covered her with a sheet.

She looked around but didn't recognize where she was. "What happened?"

His brows pinched tight. "What do you remember?"

It took her a moment to process everything. "I heard Finn's voice and then yours."

"And before that?"

What did she recall? "I was thirsty and hungry. I also remember I couldn't shift. I must have been outside because I kept licking my paws to rid them of the bugs that were crawling over me."

Declan pulled her close, and his warmth brought her such comfort. As much as she wanted to stay in his arms forever, she needed a shower.

"I have to clean up."

He slipped off the bed and held out his hand. When Chelsea stood, her legs collapsed. A second later, she was in Declan's arms. "You better let me take care of you."

Normally, she would have balked at letting someone do so much for her, but right now, she needed help. "Okay."

To her delight, the bathroom had a shower as well as a bathtub.

"Which would you prefer?" Declan asked.

"How about a bath?" He set her on the edge and ran the water. "How did you find me?" she asked.

He explained how he'd been so desperate that he appealed to the Four Sisters of Fate for their help.

"They're the ones who helped Finn free Kaleena, right?"

"Yes." He told her how he'd found her with the help from one of the white lighters who'd been imprisoned with Kaleena. "The problem was that Sanditra was so powerful that she paralyzed me before I could free you."

"Sanditra? No, it was Sabrina."

"One in the same. That's a story for another time."

At first she couldn't imagine how one person could change into another, but then she remembered how the Changelings, who were mutated werewolves who lived in Silver Lake, could alter their appearance during the red moon. "Then what happened?"

"Angelique somehow learned of your location, which led to both Thane and me fighting to take her down. I asked Finn to take you back here while I fought Sanditra. It was ugly. First, Thane saved me from sure death, and then afterward I was almost killed again. Thank the heavens that Angelique was able to get inside my body and heal me. I don't know how else to explain it."

"Inside your body? I've never heard of anything like that before."

"Me neither. What matters is that you are safe."

The tub filled with water, and Declan placed her into it. Chelsea sighed. "That feels wonderful."

Declan grabbed the bar of soap and washed her arms and legs but avoided her breasts. "I won't break if you touch me everywhere."

He tapped her nose. "You might not break, but there's no telling what I might do. You have no idea how crazy I've been trying to find you."

She reached out and grabbed his arm. "Thank you. For everything."

"You're welcome."

She sat up, the cool air puckering her nipples. "What about the shifters I saw in the back of the shelter? They each had the same silver collar on them. Did you find them?"

"Not yet."

Her heart sank. "You said that woman who took me is dead?"

"Very."

"What if she is the only one who knows where the imprisoned shifters are being held? We need to find them."

He ran a hand down her head. "Right now, you need to rest. Don't worry, we'll find them. Stick and Marty are still around, and I have a feeling they know more than they are telling."

She slumped down into the water again. "Let's hope so."

Declan pulled the handheld showerhead from the wall, warmed the water, and then ran it through her hair. Being pampered after what she'd been through was an incredible luxury.

While he washed her hair, she cleaned the rest of her body. Her neck was tender, probably because of the collar, but the rest of her had healed well. Damn dark witch, or rather dark lighter. Her admiration for Kaleena grew. Apparently, Chelsea had only been gone a few days, whereas Kaleena had been incarcerated a lot longer.

"Did you help heal me?"

"I tried, but then I found something—or someone inside you."

She stilled. "Oh, Declan. I just learned that I was pregnant and didn't have the chance to tell you before I was trapped."

"That's good to know. Do you remember anything that happened right after you stepped in the trap?"

She scoured her brain. "Marty showed up."

"Marty?"

"I thought it odd that he was in the woods near my house, but he took my leg out of the clamp after I was shot with something." Her hand went to her neck. "After that, it's more or less a blank."

"When you were shot, was Stick nearby?"

She lifted one shoulder. "I don't know."

"It's not important now. You need to finish healing."

She nodded. "I hope I remember at some point. It might help us find the others."

"Leave that to us."

"Fine." Or not.

Once Chelsea was clean, Declan helped her stand. With her hands planted on the wall, he rinsed her. Her wolf was going crazy with need, but even she understood she was too weak and needed to rest more. Tomorrow would hopefully be different.

Chapter Twenty-One

C HELSEA CRACKED OPEN an eye, and the unfamiliar surroundings took her by surprise until she remembered Declan had saved her. After that, all she remembered was him bathing her and then carrying her to bed. She must have fallen asleep before her head hit the pillow, because she didn't recall saying goodnight. As a matter of fact, she wasn't even sure Declan slept beside her.

Easing out of bed, she stood but then had to wait for the head rush to go away before walking to the bathroom. With no clock nearby, she had no idea of the time. Because of the glow behind the curtains, she assumed it was morning.

On the bathroom counter sat an unwrapped toothbrush, a tube of toothpaste, and a few other toiletries. Where was this place? Had he taken her to a hotel? She'd forgotten to ask him yesterday.

She'd just finished washing up when someone knocked on her door, and she jerked.

"Chelsea, you okay?" Declan asked as he opened the door.

She let out a breath and stepped out of the bathroom, feeling better than she had in a while. "Yes. Good morning."

He had a small satchel in his hand. "Good morning to you. How are you feeling?"

"Much better, thanks to you."

He set the bag on the bed. "I thought you might like some clothes."

Declan was wonderful. Why couldn't he be her real mate? "You are so sweet." Chelsea waved a hand as she looked inside the bag and found the clothes in there that she'd left at her house before her last run. "What is this place?"

"It's the Sinclair safe house. Actually, it's situated next to the Sinclair Mines. We have hidden entry points, so no one can find you."

"I think Finn mentioned this place once."

"Probably. Kaleena came here to heal after her ordeal. Why don't you get dressed, and then we can find something to eat? Looking at you naked has my mind going in the wrong direction."

She stepped closer and ran a finger down his chest. "Would that be so bad?"

He clasped her hand in his, and heat raced through her.

"I am not indulging in mind-blowing sex until you've eaten, and I'm convinced you are completely healed." His glowing eyes and flashing red scales under his skin assured her he missed her as much as she had missed him.

"Fine, though I admit I am famished, I can promise you I am fine now."

He smiled then patted her butt. "Get dressed."

She stuck her tongue out at him.

After they ate, she waited until he relaxed a bit before broaching the next topic. "Since I'm feeling really good, and considering that Sanditra is dead, I'd really like to go back to the cabin." She held up a hand. "Not that this place isn't awesome, but I want my routine back. It might help me remember a few things."

He smiled. "Okay, and I'll even give you a lift there."

"Yes!" She pumped her fist, and Declan laughed, something she bet he hadn't done in a while. "If you play your cards right, I might let you shower at my place." Though she had begun to think of the cabin as *their* place, and the idea of him naked had her wolf humming.

He dragged a hand down his jaw. "I guess I could use a bit of cleaning up."

If he had showered when she was asleep, she'd seen no evidence of the towel he'd used. "Did you sleep next to me last night?"

"I did, but I like getting up early."

"You didn't wake me because you were worried that I needed extra rest?"

"Yes." After they cleared their dishes, Declan escorted her outside. The sky was a brilliant blue and the air clean. "Ready for your ride?" he asked.

"Always."

One minute he was in his human form and the next, he was an incredibly magnificent dragon. Something seemed different about him though, but before she could figure it out, Declan scooped her up into his claws and soared upward.

Being safely in his embrace was a heady feeling, but the ride was over too soon. Declan landed, and right before he shifted, light glinted off a scale near his heart. It was white and pulsating.

He shifted and smiled. "Is something wrong?" he asked.

"No, but one of your scales is white." Chelsea pointed to his heart. "It was right about here. I don't remember that before."

"It's new. That's how I found you." He explained how the Four Sisters had taken the hair from her brush and combined it with other things to make a scale that acted like a tracking device only for her.

She stepped up to him. "Did I mention that you are an amazing man?"

"Is that so?" Declan wrapped an arm around her waist.

"Yes, and I'd like to thank you properly, just as soon as you shower." She ran a finger down his out-of-control bristle.

He laughed, released her, and then dug his hand into his pocket to retrieve the door key.

Once open, she stepped inside and inhaled. The air was a little musty, but it was where she belonged. "Home, sweet home."

"Before I indulge in what I've been dreaming about for days, I will clean up first, as you so nicely suggested."

Chelsea chuckled. "I don't think my wolf could handle seeing you naked and not do something. While you shower, I'll just check to make sure nothing spoiled in the fridge during my absence."

"I'll be quick." As soon as Declan headed down the hallway, Chelsea went into the kitchen to find out what smelled.

She quickly located the offending piece of meat and tossed it in the trashcan outside. Less than ten minutes later, a very handsome Declan came out of the bathroom barefoot and wearing only jeans. He looked so yummy.

"Feel better?" she asked as she moved toward him.

"Definitely."

Declan framed her face with his palms and leaned over. When their lips met, her wolf begged to come out and play, and boy did she beg. *Be good*, she commanded.

It's been too long, her wolf whined.

Declan's teeth sharpened, and his talons poked out of his skin.

"Chelsea."

His panted plea nearly melted her bones. Just as she was about to take off his pants, someone knocked on the front door. She stiffened.

"It's not a shifter," he said.

That much she could tell. "It could be another dark lighter."

His cheer evaporated. Declan let go of her and strode over to the door and pulled it open. "Poppy?"

From his shocked tone, she was the last person he expected. Chelsea rushed to the front. The only Poppy she'd heard about had been one of the Four Sisters who'd helped Declan find her. This woman was pretty with nearly white blonde hair, tinted purple at the ends.

The newcomer smiled. "May I come in?" Poppy faced her and held out her hand. "I'm so glad to see you're okay."

"Poppy is one of the Four Sisters who removed your collar."

Chelsea shook her hand. "Thank you for all your help."

"My pleasure."

He motioned she come in. "What can we do for you?" Declan asked.

She patted his arm. "I need to talk with you two. Let's sit."

That sounded ominous. Declan and Chelsea sat on the sofa with

Poppy across from them.

"As you know, a shifter only has one mate in a lifetime," she said.

Hearing those words spoken out loud deflated Chelsea's heart and caused her chin to tremble. "Yes," Chelsea mumbled her response, while Declan said nothing.

Poppy looked over at him. "After you gave us a hair sample in which to build your scale, we could tell that Chelsea was pregnant."

"You could? I just found out myself." Declan looked over at Chelsea and smiled.

"The Guardians have done a lot for all of Tarradon, and it would be a shame not to bring the first born of this generation into the Guardian fold."

Declan clutched Chelsea's hand. "What are you saying?"

She inhaled. "Once my sisters and I realized that Chelsea was pregnant with your child, we contacted Fate."

Her heart beat so fast, she feared she might do damage to their unborn child.

"The baby is mine, but how did you know?" Declan asked.

Poppy's lips lifted slightly. "We know."

"Go on," he urged, his grip tightening.

"Fate has decided that you are meant to follow the path you are on together." She held up a hand. "Mind you, this might never happen to anyone else again, so be grateful."

Declan's eyes widened while Chelsea's teared up. "I am, but are you saying that Chelsea and I are really mates?"

Poppy clapped. "Yes." She leaned forward. "We drew straws to see who would be the bearer of good news—and I won." She sighed. "I'm a sucker for a good love story."

It was true. Really true. She and Declan could be together forever. Chelsea looked over at him, and her heart hitched at the joy in his eyes. She had to swipe away her own tears.

Declan jumped up from the sofa and rubbed his hands together. "I don't know what to say or how to thank you."

Poppy stood. "I don't think you need any words to mate." She winked—and then she disappeared.

Laughter bubbled up inside of Chelsea. She rose to her feet and threw her arms around his neck. "It's too good to be true. Fate gave you a second chance."

"Fate gave me you, along with our baby." Declan lifted his chin. "Just for the record, I knew we were mates from the moment I met you."

She lightly punched his arm. "I'm calling bullshit!"

He grinned. "Okay, I felt as if we were mates, but I was told Fate only granted us one mate in a lifetime."

"I was taught that too, but at the time I didn't know you'd had a mate. It was why I asked Finn to bring me to Tarradon. You can imagine how devastated I was when Kaleena told me about Bess."

He stroked her face. "Yet you stayed."

"Because I thought maybe Fate was wrong."

He smiled. "You were right. Kind of." Declan lifted her up and carried her to the bedroom. "I've waited for this moment for a long time."

"Me too. I love you, Declan Sinclair."

He grinned. "I love you too."

With their gazes locked, he carried her into the bedroom, and then slowly lowered her down to sit on the edge of the bed.

Declan stood in front of her as she unfastened and pushed his jeans down his legs. "Where are your briefs?" she asked.

"I was hoping I wouldn't need them."

She raised her eyebrows. "Confident, weren't you?"

He stepped back and tugged off his pants. Blue sparks shot off her arms in anticipation of what was to come. This was it! The one moment she'd been waiting for her whole life. Chelsea silently thanked Fate for allowing them to be together.

Reaching out, she grabbed his hips and pulled him closer. She licked her lips and then drew his dick deep into her mouth. "Mmm."

He groaned. Declan clutched a handful of her hair and wrapped it around his fist. On the first tug, Chelsea was tempted to rise up and bite his neck since she wanted Declan more than life itself, but rushing would make their amazing journey end too soon. She continued to swirl her tongue around his hard shaft, loving how it made her feel powerful and in control. When she cupped his balls, he leaned back.

"Stop, I don't want to finish this way. I want you so bad; I have to be inside you," he whispered.

Chelsea stood and motioned him to get up on the bed.

Naked, Declan sat down, scooted back, and leaned against the headboard. Like a cat stalking her prey, Chelsea hopped onto the bed but kept her distance. With her gaze focused on his face, she lifted off her shirt and then slowly eased down the bra straps, loving how his eyes sparkled, and his scales flashed red. Once she let the bra fall, she hooked her thumbs in the waistband of her pants and stopped, wanting to drive him crazy.

"You're taking your sweet time. Speed it up, darlin', or I'll have to rip the rest of your clothes off you."

She laughed. "Not on your life. I'm enjoying this, and don't you dare think of ripping anything off me. I have just enough panties right now and no spares."

Declan crossed his arms and grinned. "I will buy you all the panties you want, better yet, maybe I won't. I like you naked, if you ever get there, woman."

Chelsea snorted as she pulled down her shorts and then her panties. The shoes she'd ditched a while ago.

Declan hissed in a breath. "Geezus, you are a sight for sore eyes."

Chelsea edged closer. As soon as she was within reach, he drew her near, forcing her to straddle him. When she rubbed against his cock, her blue sparks turned into a big blue cocoon.

"Someone's excited," Declan said.

She ground against his erection. "You have no room to talk. Check your hands—or rather what used to be hands. And if you haven't noticed, you're as bright as a flashing neon light."

As if he decided there would be no more small talk, he drew her head to his and kissed her hard. Every one of her senses exploded with passionate desire. Their tongues entwined, and strong spikes of need shot through her veins.

Needing air, she broke the contact and leaned back. Declan zeroed in on her breasts. "Magnificent." He cupped them both as he kissed around the edges before he flicked his thumbs over her nipples. Waves of delight spread throughout her body.

Even though all these blue sparks were new to her, Declan sure was able to draw them out of her with ease. She placed her hands on his head, reveling in the way his short hair bristled against her palms. Declan moved his mouth to her nipples, taking her closer to her climax. She wanted him so badly.

"Harder," she demanded.

Declan delivered, drawing out every erotic impulse in her body. She slid her pussy across his cock, thrilling at how his hardness could take her higher and higher.

He nipped at her nipple, causing a brief shot of pain. As if he could already sense what she was experiencing, he swirled his tongue around the tip to ease the ache. The alternating sensations of slight pain with the euphoric highs nearly undid her.

"I'm ready," she panted.

Without waiting for his consent, Chelsea slipped a hand between them and grabbed his cock. Keeping it upright, she aimed it straight into her. After today, they would be one, united in both heart and soul.

Declan looked up at her. Swirls of gold and red streamed through his teal eyes. "Yes!"

It was as if he was saying yes to a lifetime together. Chelsea closed her eyes and slid all the way down, absorbing their sensual scents and loving the way her body adapted to his large size.

Heat sizzled throughout her veins when she lifted up and then dropped back down on him once more. Declan ran his hands down her back and cupped her butt. When he squeezed, her heart pounded harder. Maybe it was the extra hormones coursing through her, but each thrust became more amazing than the last.

Declan pressed his cheek against her neck and ran his tongue from her shoulder blade up to her ear. "I need you so much, Chelsea."

I need you more. She would have said it out loud, but the words didn't form.

Wanting to be one with him, she lowered her lips to the spot where his neck met his shoulder. Her teeth sharpened, and her blue glow surrounded them. It was time. Chelsea wanted to love him forever and love him unconditionally.

Declan grabbed hold of her hips and lifted her up slightly. As he pressed his fangs against her tender skin, he drove up into her. Together, they sunk their teeth into each other. That union caused a tsunami of lust and desire that encompassed her body and transformed her. It was almost as if she could feel his dragon entering her body and taking over her soul.

Her vision turned white, and her nails sharpened into claws. It was happening. The joining. The mating. The joy of it all.

They both lifted their heads at the same time and gently licked away the evidence of their mating. Once finished, her body continued to sing with joy. She doubted anything could be better.

Declan lifted his head and leaned back. "Are you okay?"

How could he ask that question? She sat up and smiled. "More than okay. Anyone up for another round?"

He laughed. "Life with you will be non-stop fun."

"You got that right."

Chapter Twenty-Two

"WHEN DO I get to shift into a big bad dragon?" Chelsea asked.

Declan wanted to give her everything in this world, but he needed to be sure that shifting wouldn't hurt the baby. "Your body is used to being a wolf, but a dragon is a whole different experience. I want to talk to a few people to make sure it's safe."

Chelsea flopped down on the sofa. "I miss going out on runs."

"You can still do that."

She looked up and smiled. "Really? Would you come with me?"

Kaleena had inherited the ability to change into a wolf when she'd mated with Finn, so hopefully, Declan would be just as lucky. "I'd love that."

"Afterward, I want to talk about my job," she said.

"You can't go back to the shelter."

"Why not?"

He blew out a breath. "Seriously? You found captured shifters in the back of the office. Just because neither Finn nor I sensed them there, doesn't mean that Stick isn't involved. There's nothing to stop him from trying to silence you."

She waved a hand. "I don't think he'd do that."

"I'm not taking any chances. We'll find you another job. Now that Sabrina is dead, there's a vacancy at the vet's office where she worked."

Chelsea scrunched up her face. "That's almost sick." She twisted toward him. "In all honesty, I've been thinking about going back to school to be a vet."

Declan dropped down in front of her. "I love that idea. We have some universities here."

"Do you think I could get in? All of my experience and credits come from Earth."

He smiled, happy he could help her. "I imagine I can talk to a few people."

"The Guardians have that much pull?"

"Few people know we are Guardians, but the Sinclair name is well-known."

Chelsea grinned and then patted her stomach. "I'm glad our child will have some advantages."

"That he will."

"He? How can you be certain it's a boy?"

Declan didn't care just as long as both mother and child were healthy. "Just guessing since my family is predominantly male."

"Then it's time for a female."

He laughed and stood. "Maybe it is. Come on. Let's see if I can master shifting into a wolf. I'm not sure my dragon will be willing to give up control though."

She stood. "He will if he wants to catch me." Chelsea unbuttoned her shirt.

Declan reached out and clasped her hands. "You don't have to undress anymore. I thought Finn told you."

"He did. Sorry. It's an old habit."

"Come on. Shift into your wolf. If your clothes rip, I'll buy you new ones."

Chelsea wrapped her arms around his neck. "Did I mention that I love you?"

He laughed. "Not in the last ten minutes." They both stepped outside and headed down the trail. "Any words of wisdom?" he asked.

"I honestly have no idea what to say. I was hoping you could just tell your body which animal you want to become and voilà, you'd be a wolf. If that doesn't work, when he sees me take off, your dragon won't be able to stand not catching me. I'm hoping he'll force the shift. Ready?"

This would be a total downer if he failed. Declan would never live it down. "Go."

One second, she was his beautiful mate and the next, she was a sleek wolf—one who looked a lot better than the captured wolf of a few days ago. Chelsea's fur was a shiny dark brown with light gray mixed in, and her snout had the cutest white patch in the center. She scurried down the path.

Follow her, he commanded his wolf, though he felt strange talking to an animal he'd never met.

Chelsea was almost out of sight when Declan started running on his own. After a few steps, his bones cracked, and his vision blurred. He almost stopped because the discomfort surprised him. Without warning, he was on all fours, his face close to the ground. While he always had a great sense of smell while in his dragon form, this dirt smelled sweeter, possibly because he was so close to it.

"*Chelsea*," he telepathed, hoping that channel of communication had formed.

"*Declan?*"

"*Yes, I'm coming.*"

To his delight, a small patch of white flickered on his chest. Instead of it being a scale, his fur was flashing. The Four Sisters of Fate had thought of everything.

When he rounded the corner, Chelsea was sitting on her haunches, panting. She was such a beautiful animal. He had no idea what he looked like other than his paws were black with some brown woven in. Without a mirror, he couldn't know what he looked like.

"*I see you made it,*" she sent out mentally.

He caught the humor in her voice. "*Race you to the waterfall.*"

She howled. "*You're on.*"

Declan took off and passed her before she rose up and turned around. Being in the lead was a natural place for him. He charged down the path, loving the feel of the ground on his paws. This new perspective was intriguing. As much as he wanted to stop and check things out, he had a race to win.

Leaves rustled to his left. When he looked over, he caught sight of Chelsea dashing across downed logs and darting over the underbrush. She was taking a shortcut. Sneaky one. Her way was shorter, but it was fraught with possible delays.

The river with the waterfall wasn't far head, so he turned on his speed. He tried to extend his wings to take off, only to remember he was still a wolf. He could have changed into his dragon form, but the forest was too dense for him to be effective. From the amount of leaves crunching, Chelsea must be struggling a bit to reach the destination before him.

Two minutes later, he broke over the ridge and spotted the stream. He charged down the path and made it to the river mere seconds before she did.

Needing to be in his human form, he closed his eyes and pictured his human self. Seconds later, he transformed, though the process would take some getting used to. Thankfully, he was still dressed in his jeans, shirt, and boots. Chelsea stopped at his feet and looked up at him.

"Wish me luck I don't end up naked," she telepathed.

"If you do, I promise not to be disappointed."

She spun around and became human in two seconds. She looked down and ran her hand down her shirt front. "It really is magic. I love it."

"How about taking them off and going for a cool swim in the falls?"

"Now you're talking."

"DO YOU REMEMBER anything?" Tory asked Chelsea.

She sat at a large table at the Wing's Bar with Kaleena, Tory, Nessa, Lily, and Greer for a girls' night out. This celebration had been Kaleena's idea.

"You mean about what happened after I was captured?"

Tory nodded.

"Some things—like waking up in a cage and seeing Sabrina, who I found out later had the ability to transform into that dark lighter Sanditra. I think she must have put a spell on me that made me forget much of it." Back home, that had happened to her cousin and her mate. Thankfully, a goddess was able to retrieve their memory for them. In all honesty, Chelsea wasn't sure she wanted to remember it all.

Kaleena held up her glass. "Before we start celebrating, I want to have a toast to the first baby Guardian!"

Heat raced up Chelsea's face at all the good wishes. "Thanks. Declan and I are both ecstatic."

"Are you hoping for a boy or a girl?" Nessa asked.

"Both? Okay, not at once, but I like the idea of having a lot of kids and a lot of animals."

They all talked about what life would be like having to balance their jobs and children. Declan's work could create some long hours, but he'd already promised he would be around to help out as much as possible. He wanted to be a hands-on dad. Momma Sinclair had been the first to volunteer for grandbaby duty, saying she'd help out whenever she was needed.

"Have you tried shifting into a dragon yet?" Tory asked, excitement lacing her voice.

"No, but Declan shifted into his wolf. We ran the trails to the waterfall. It was so cool. Declan is very excited about his ability to be both animals."

Kaleena nodded. "I know I love it, and Finn loves being able to fly."

"I want to try, but Declan made me promise to wait until we see a doctor to be sure there won't be any issues with the baby."

"It's better to be safe." Tory leaned forward. "Any progress on finding those missing shifters you saw in the back of the shelter? Finn told us he didn't sense them anywhere."

"No, but I'm not allowed to be involved even if they do find them," Chelsea said. "Declan thinks that I might still be in danger." She refrained from rolling her eyes.

"From Stick?"

"Yes, and Marty. If Declan was protective before, he's even more protective now that I'm pregnant."

Kaleena chuckled. "That's my brother, though if I were pregnant, I'm not sure Finn would let me leave the condo."

They all laughed.

"What about Angelique?" Nessa asked. "She found you, so maybe she can find the missing shifters."

"I think she was able to detect Sanditra for some reason. From what Declan said, there seemed to be a history between those two, but I don't know what it was."

For the rest of the time, they talked about their work and how things were going in general. As much as Chelsea wanted to remember every detail of her capture in the hopes of having a clue where the captured shifters might be held, she probably should just focus on getting into school and preparing to be a mother. It made sense to leave the battles to Declan and the Guardians.

DECLAN WASN'T RECEIVING any reading of anxiety from Chelsea, but he wanted her home. Sure, she was with his sisters and cousins, but he still worried about her. Sanditra might be dead, but Stick might suspect that Chelsea had seen something at the shelter that she shouldn't have. He couldn't be certain the captured shifters and Chelsea's kidnapping were related, especially since Sabrina/Sanditra claimed she only wanted Kaleena, but the fact Chelsea was wearing a silver collar and the shifters Chelsea had seen wore silver collars too, implied Stick might be involved.

If Declan had to guess, the Royals never forgave Sanditra for letting Kaleena escape from their prison in the first place. This might have been her way to save face. Now, she'd never be absolved.

As terrible as that time had been for Declan—not knowing what was happening to his sister—it ended up to be for the best. She'd been able to contact Finn on Earth who'd had the courage to believe in the love of a mate and who'd found his way through a portal to Tarradon.

And now, Declan was mated to his twin sister. He sighed. Life was good, though it would be even better once Chelsea came home. He needed her. As if he'd conjured her up, Chelsea's car pulled down their driveway. Declan jumped up and peered out the window. While he didn't like her out alone, he understood that having friends would keep her happy. His job at the mine, together with being a Guardian, would take him away from her often enough, and he wanted her to know she wasn't alone on Tarradon.

The front door opened, and the love of his life stepped in. He had felt guilty at first at loving Chelsea when Bess had been his first mate, but after he and Chelsea mated, Bess had come to him in a dream and told him she was pleased he'd been able to move on. Having her blessing meant the world to him.

Chelsea smiled. "Hi," she said.

"How did it go?"

"We had fun. You have the best family."

He gathered her in his arms and kissed her. "I do at that. I missed you."

She leaned back and placed a hand on his chest. "I'm here now."

"That you are. How are you feeling? Are you too tired to enjoy what I have to offer?"

Chelsea laughed. "Never. Even if I wanted to sleep, I don't think my wolf or my dragon would let me."

"Has your dragon spoken to you yet?" His wolf had been in a constant conversation with his dragon about how much they needed her.

"If you are asking if they are begging me to ravish you, then yes."

"I like animal battles like that."

He swooped her up in his arms, ready to spend the rest of the night making love to his mate.

Chapter Twenty-Three

LAST NIGHT HAD been amazing. Declan had driven her crazy, kissing her slowly and then sucking on her nipples and pussy until she was ready to explode. Chelsea tried to reciprocate, but he seemed determined to drive her wild first. Even though the girls had warned her that after she mated her desires would increase, Chelsea hadn't believed them. Now she did.

Chelsea sipped her morning coffee as she relived their glorious night together. It had been so cool when not only her blue sparks had flown off her body, she'd actually glowed light blue from the inside. Declan said that meant she'd have black scales, scattered with pretty blue ones. She couldn't wait until she shifted. Blue was her favorite color.

Declan had left early this morning. He, along with Finn and several of the other Guardians, were on a mission to find the missing shifters. Chelsea could only hope that Sanditra hadn't been the one responsible for taking them. Now that she was dead, these caged souls might never be freed.

Considering how strong-willed Sanditra had been, she might have mentally controlled Stick and Marty to do her bidding. Hell, they might not remember where she was keeping them—assuming they both had been involved. Wherever those shifters were, she hoped someone was watching over them.

Once she finished breakfast, Chelsea pulled out her laptop and began checking out colleges to find the perfect school for veterinarian medicine. After an hour of searching, she'd found two. The question was whether any of her Earth credits would be accepted.

She thought about calling Declan to see if he could find out something about reciprocity between Earth and Tarradon, but she didn't want to disturb him, especially since he was on a mission dear to her heart—finding those poor shifters.

Before she could figure out her next move, someone knocked on her front door. Chelsea stiffened. She couldn't tell if it was a shifter or not, which was odd, but she chalked it up to the fact that her body was trying to incorporate two animal beings at once.

Even knowing that Sanditra was dead, she cautiously glanced out the living room window. The only vehicle in her drive belonged to her. From her vantage point, she couldn't see who was at the door. Darn.

"Who is it?" she called out.

No one answered. Then what sounded like a bird's beak rapped on her door, and her body sagged. It hadn't been a knock at all—just some woodpecker. She certainly didn't need him to drill a hole in the wood.

Wanting to shoo him away, she pulled open the door, and the damn thing flew in.

"Oh, no you don't. Get out of here. Scram."

As much as she liked all animals, it wouldn't do the bird any good to be cooped up in the cabin. The bird flew toward the door. Right as it passed her, it shifted into a man.

Chelsea was so stunned that she couldn't move. Never had she heard of a bird shifter. "Marty? What...what are you doing here?" This couldn't be good.

He stepped back and withdrew a gun from his jacket pocket. She froze. Chelsea had never had a gun pointed at her before. Probably because she'd watched so many cop shows back home that she raised her arms.

"Where's Sanditra? And how did you get away from her?"

He must not know she was dead, but clearly he knew Sanditra had kept Chelsea captive. A thousand responses tumbled through her mind. Maybe Marty wasn't out to kill her. All he wanted was information. Should she tell him the truth or lie?

"I don't know. But Declan does." It wasn't as if she was throwing her mate under the bus, but he could squash this little bird a lot better than she could.

"You know nothing then?" Marty asked.

"Chelsea, are you okay?" Declan's voice filtered into her mind, and it took her a moment to remember they could communicate telepathically.

"Marty is at the cabin—and he has a gun pointed at me."

"Hold on. I'll be there in five."

It took a second to remember Marty's question. "I don't remember much after you helped me escape from that trap. I remember waking up outside, tied to something. You weren't there then, but I imagine you would know more than me."

"Sanditra was there, right?"

"I couldn't say. It was all a blur, but I do know the next time I woke up, I was inside a house, and Sabrina, or rather Sanditra, was there."

He paced in front of her. Chelsea lowered her arms and remained still, trying to figure out her next move. She could shift and attack, but he did have a gun.

Marty swung back around to face her. "How did you get away?"

"At the time of my rescue I was unconscious. When I woke up, Declan told me that he and a few others had found me. He never said how. Apparently, several of the dragon shifters took on Sanditra. I think she might be dead."

Marty's face seemed to change colors right in front of her, and his gun hand wavered. "Go outside."

"Why?" Her chest squeezed tight, though she'd have a better chance of attacking him in the open.

His lip curled. "Because I said so."

With his free hand, he removed a silver collar from his pocket, the same kind that she'd worn when she was captive, and her heart slammed against her rib cage. He dangled it in front of her. There was no way she'd let him take her.

Think, think.

Let me take him, her wolf said. *I can do it.*

Okay. You have one chance, so get it right.

Chelsea might not need Declan to save her after all. She nodded to the side table. "There are the keys to my car. I doubt a crow can carry a wolf."

"No, I can't."

While fighting wasn't her thing, she would do whatever it took to save her child. She stepped out onto the porch. Without warning, Marty kicked her square in the back, and she went sailing through the air. Even though she stretched out her arms to brace for impact, she landed face down in the dirt. Anger welled inside her so hard it nearly short-circuited her brain. The fucker would pay for that. Her knees and elbows stung from the abrasion, but other than that she seemed okay.

"Chelsea?" Declan's thoughts came out strangled. *"I'm almost there."*

She didn't want him to worry. She had everything under control. *"I'm good."*

"Get up," Marty commanded.

She rolled over, trying to catch her breath. Instead of standing, she rose to all fours. Two seconds later, she was in her wolf form. Not wanting Marty to have time to react, she charged. Just as she leapt at him, he fired his gun twice in rapid succession. Hot piercing pain sliced through one leg and then the other, causing her to miss her mark. When she landed two feet from Marty, her legs collapsed, and her snout smashed into a rock. Shit.

Her wolf would heal her, but not in time for her to escape. Fury ripped through her so fast that her body nearly exploded. The next thing she knew, her limbs seemed to be splitting apart, and her head felt like someone had attached two claws on either side of her face and were pulling in opposite directions. When she finally focused, she was eye level with the top of the cabin. What the hell?

Marty dropped his gun and the silver collar, and then rushed toward the car. Confusion and elation blasted her at once. Holy shit. She'd shifted into a dragon! Chelsea hadn't commanded the change, but her dragon must have known that the only way to defeat this ass was to change form. Sure, her legs hurt somewhat, but since she was mostly wing, the injuries seemed small.

Extending her claws like she's seen so many dragons do, she caught Marty before he got in the car. With a quick flap of her wings, she soared upward, not worrying about whether or not she could fly. Out of the corner of her eye, she spotted another dragon racing toward her. The smattering of red scales told her it was Declan.

Right before he reached her, Marty slipped from her grasp. He sailed downward and then shifted into his avian form. *"Marty just escaped!"*

"I'll stop him," Declan telepathed.

A huge stream of fire shot from Declan's mouth, and just like that, Marty was no more. Chelsea was so relieved that she totally forgot to flap her wings. As she tumbled downward, her instincts kicked in, and she beat them once more. After leveling off, she turned around and headed back to the cabin. Declan pulled up alongside her a second later.

She shifted back into her human form and dropped to the ground. Okay, that had been a big mistake. While the bullet holes had closed up, blood covered both of her legs.

"Chelsea!" Declan picked her up and rushed her into the house. "He shot you?"

"Yes, but my wolf, or maybe it was my dragon, kind of healed me."

He set her down on the sofa. "Not enough. How about shifting into your wolf again? Between the two of us, you'll be good as new in no time."

"Can I have a kiss first?"

He grinned. "You can have anything you want. I can't tell you how scared I was when I felt your pain."

She reached up and stroked his face. "You are my world."

"And you are mine. Now I need to heal you, so do as I say."

Happy that she was safe with Declan, she shifted into her wolf form. He began by placing his hands on her stomach. He'd told her how he'd been able to sense a second life force inside her. Because of this recent event, he was probably making sure the baby was fine.

"Our child took it in stride," he announced with a smile.

"She's strong," Chelsea shot back.

"She? Never mind. I don't even want to know. She or he, I will be happy the moment our child is born."

Heat shot through her when he touched her legs, but even her wolf seemed impressed with the way the pain was dissipating. Between the two of them, her strength slowly returned.

Chelsea roused to the smell of coffee, not aware she'd fallen asleep. She shifted and sat up.

"How are you feeling?" Declan asked with a smile.

She glanced down at her legs, and then ran her hands down them to where only two faint marks remained. "It's remarkable. I know my wolf can heal me, but she isn't that good."

He laughed. "You not only have your wolf to help, but your dragon is also very powerful. I just added a touch of magic to make the two work together. Angelique's spell kept the baby safe, but I would suggest you keep out of harm's way from now on."

Declan placed a cup of tea on the table in front of her.

"Tea?"

"I've heard it's safer for the baby."

She smiled. "Thank you. Just so you know, it wasn't as if I asked for Marty to stop by."

"Why did you let him in? You had to have suspected he might be dangerous."

"I didn't let him in. Not really." Chelsea explained about hearing the bird tapping and then how he just flew in.

"Stick told me that Marty was a crow shifter. I'm sorry I forgot to mention it to you."

"It's okay. I didn't sense he was a shifter. I might have opened the door anyway even if I knew."

Declan nodded. "Did he say what he wanted?"

"He wanted to find Sanditra."

"Ah."

She went on to explain the subsequent events. "If you hadn't fried the bastard when you did, I would have killed him." This conversation seemed to worry him anew so she changed the subject. "Did you make any progress on finding the shifters?"

Declan leaned back against the sofa. "No, but the men are still looking."

"What about Stick? What does he say?"

"That he knows nothing about anything, though he admits there were animals that he was treating in the backroom. He claimed the silver collars you noticed were merely monitoring devices so he could tell if any were in respiratory distress."

"Bullshit. Marty had one of those *monitoring devices* with him— to use on me. He dropped it when I shifted into my dragon form. What did Stick say happened to these animals?"

"He said all but two recovered from their infection, and that the rest had already been adopted. The two ill ones are with a different vet—one with more sophisticated equipment—or so Stick claims."

"That's a total lie. Have you checked with your cousin Anderson? If someone in my family went missing, I'd report it."

Declan drank his coffee. "I asked, but there haven't been any new reports of missing men. I would imagine that if Stick, Marty, or Sanditra abducted these men or women, they might have been ones without a family."

"That would be smart. What are you going to do now?" she asked.

"We'll regroup in a little while to come up with a plan. In the meantime, I'd like you to consider something."

He sounded ominous. "What?"

Declan picked up her hands. "I'm worried that Stick might come after you—or send someone else to harm you."

She sagged. "I'm not staying in the safe house."

"I know. What would you say, to visiting your parents?"

Joy and adrenaline surged through her. "Really? Of course I'd love to see them, but I'd miss you too much."

He leaned over and gave her a rather chaste kiss. It was as if he feared she wasn't ready for more.

"But you'll go?" he asked.

"I will if you come with me."

He dragged a knuckle down her cheek. Chelsea knew him well enough to know he would if he could. "How about if I take you there? I'll stay a few hours, meet the parents, and then head back. I would love to get to know them, but I do have a few people to save here."

She appreciated his compromise. "How long would I need to stay? Being away from you for a long time is not an option. It's hard enough not being with you every hour of every day."

He curled a finger around her hair. "I do love you."

"And I love you, which is the problem."

Declan lowered his chin. "Chelsea, stop stalling. I would feel a lot better knowing you were safe."

She loved safety too. "I do have our child to think about."

"That's a yes then?"

Unable to come up with a logical objection, she nodded. "Yes, but I need to shower first. I'm not fit company for anyone."

"Go ahead, and I'll help you pack."

She saluted him and stood, feeling almost one-hundred percent.

Chapter Twenty-Four

WHILE DECLAN ENJOYED meeting Chelsea's parents, he needed to end this mess with the missing shifters once and for all, so he and Chelsea could get on with their lives. After a tearful goodbye on Chelsea's part, he left.

Within minutes, he was in the SinCas hallway, striding into the conference room. Finn, Thane, Griffin, Tory, and his dad were seated around the table, coffee in hand, chatting up a storm.

He'd already contacted Finn and told him that Chelsea and he had gone to Earth, and Finn couldn't have been more pleased.

They looked up. "How did the trip go?" Finn asked.

Declan smiled. "It would be an understatement to say your parents were happy to see her. They also kept asking when you and Kaleena would return for a visit."

"Soon."

"Declan?" his father said with a reprimanding tone.

Finn tossed him a quick smile. "We'll chat later."

Declan nodded and took a seat. "What do we know?" he asked.

"We canvassed the area for hours," his father said. "We didn't find shit."

Declan snapped his fingers. "I should have thought about this sooner, but I couldn't detect Sanditra's shifter signature before or after she shifted."

"A powerful dark lighter can cloak better than anyone," his father shot back.

"Could Sanditra have created a spell to dampen their shifter signature to make it harder to find them?" Thane asked.

"It's possible, but it's not like we can ask her," Declan said. "Chelsea told me that she could tell those in the cages were shifters, but I should have asked if their total signature had the strength of one or ten."

"If Sanditra was the Royals most powerful dark lighter, maybe Stick took them to the castle. For all we know, the Royals paid him for delivery already," his father said.

"Do we have a clue what the Royals want them for?" Griffin asked.

His dad shrugged. "It could be a way to increase their slave population."

Fuck. "Who would know?" Declan asked. "Certainly not aunt Teresa, our useless queen. The king keeps her in the dark when it comes to the running of the province."

"Good point."

Declan pushed back his chair. "I'm going to find Stick. I'll convince him it's in his best interest to talk."

"We already stopped by the shelter, but he wasn't there," Finn said.

Damn. "Unless he figures out a way to get through a portal, he has to be on Tarradon somewhere. I don't see him abandoning those shifters. He doesn't seem the type to leave that kind of investment behind. No, he'll be nearby. Where however is anyone's guess."

"Need any help?" Thane asked.

It would be near to impossible to search everywhere. "Sure."

Declan broke up the province into sections. It was decided that Thane would scour the forested areas while Finn would take the west half of town. Declan said he'd start with Stick's house again and then look on the east half.

"I'll ask around some vet offices to see if someone knows anything about some collared animals," Tory said.

"Great." He turned to Griffin. "You'll be the point person. Everyone, contact Griffin if you learn something. We all need to know what everyone is doing."

This was fairly standard practice for the Guardians, but for some reason, this was a more important assignment than usual. Chelsea was safe for now, but the sooner these shifters were located and Stick was out of the way, the sooner Declan could bring Chelsea home.

The group left—some by wing, others on foot. Stick lived on the edge of town, so Declan drove to his house. It didn't come as a surprise that he wasn't there. In fact, from the looks of the front lawn, Stick hadn't been back to his place in a while. The big question was, where was he?

Declan returned to his car and decided Anderson might know something.

Inside the police station, Declan found his cousin on the phone. He motioned for Declan to take a seat. Once Anderson finished his conversation, he gave him his undivided attention. Most of the time it was Anderson who was asking for the Guardians' help, not the other way around.

"What brings you here?"

Declan glanced around to make sure no one was within earshot. "I'm looking for a man by the name of Seth Parnell. He goes by the nickname of Stick."

"You mentioned him before. You thought he might be operating a shady animal shelter."

"Yes. Now I think he is involved in something bigger. Possibly kidnapping, drugging, and selling shifters as slaves."

Anderson whistled. "That is quite a big accusation. Do you have any proof?"

Declan explained what Chelsea saw, and then how she was captured and collared. "It took me, Thane, and a very powerful white lighter to bring this woman down."

"I see. How can I help?"

"I need to find this guy. He is the last link. Can you check facial recognition for him? He's got to be somewhere."

Anderson pushed back his chair. "Come with me."

Declan followed his cousin down a series of halls where they took an elevator to the basement. Inside one room was a series of about one hundred monitors. A technician was seated at a table facing the massive screens.

He turned around. "Hey, Anderson. What brings you down here?"

Anderson explained about the need to find Seth Parnell.

"I'll pull up his driver's license photo and use that for comparison purposes. It might take me a few hours to find him though."

Declan was fine with that. "Call me when you locate him."

"Will do."

He and Anderson left. "What are you going to do once you find him?" Anderson asked.

"Follow him until I learn the location of the captives. I'll call for backup if need be, and then take it from there. Parnell is a lion shifter so I don't think he'll want to fight me."

"For his sake, let's hope not."

AFTER DECLAN RETURNED to the mining office, it was five hours before Anderson called back. "What did you find out?" Declan said without bothering with a greeting.

"Hello to you too."

"Sorry."

"We found your man, Stick. He's been bar hopping. The last time he showed up on a camera was about thirty minutes ago at the Hog's Head Bar."

It figured Stick would go to a scummy place like that. "Thanks. Let me know if he moves."

"Will do."

Declan contacted Griffin and told him about the new development.

"I'll let the team know. Thane and Finn can provide backup."

Declan would never be able to explain their presence if all three waltzed in. "Fine, but tell them to keep a low profile outside."

"Will do."

Wanting to have a bit more freedom moving about, Declan headed out on foot. When he reached the Hog's Head Bar, he slipped inside. Someday, he hoped one of the Guardians mated with a white lighter who had the ability to become invisible at will. If one of their ranks could move around undetected, they could nab a lot more criminals.

Declan entered the highly offensive smelling bar. At least the dim lights helped his cause of trying to remain unnoticed.

"Hi, handsome," said a woman wearing a pair of skimpy shorts and a bra top with the Hog's Head logo on it. "Can I get you anything?"

"In a moment."

"I'm Sandy. Just let me know."

He debated asking if she'd seen Stick, but at that moment he spotted his prey. "Will do, sugar." The words burned on his lips.

Sandy disappeared. It was time for Declan to do the same. Outside, he sensed Finn and Thane and then found them leaning against the wall at the corner.

"Is he in there?" Thane asked.

"Yup."

"What's the plan?" Finn asked.

"All we can do is wait and follow him. I doubt he'll head straight to the captives, but at some point he'll have to," Declan said.

"I can take first shift," Thane said. "He doesn't know me."

That made sense. "It's nine now, so we'll do six hour shifts. Let us know once he leaves and where he ends up. I'll take the next six hours, and then Finn can follow up with the nine a.m. to three p.m. shift."

"Works for me."

With Chelsea safely on Earth and Thane watching their mark, Declan returned to the mines—a place that brought him comfort. Knowing he'd get no sleep tonight, he busied himself with work.

What with Chelsea being held captive and then helping her heal, he'd slacked off these last few days. It was time to get to work.

His cell beeped at three a.m. The message said that Stick had left the bar with some guy, and that the two had gone to an apartment complex in town. Thane gave the address and said he'd wait for Declan before heading home.

Declan pushed back his chair. He texted back: *Thanks. On my way there now.*

He found his brother outside the apartment building. "They're in apartment 423," Thane said.

"You know that how?"

"Really? I waited to see which lights turned on and then peeked in the window."

Being a dragon had a lot of advantages. "Sneaky. Get some rest. And thanks."

"Call if they do anything."

"Will do."

Once Thane left, it was a little over two hours before Stick and some guy exited the building. They looked both ways before heading to a blue four-door car that looked to be about ten years old. They slipped in and took off.

Declan contacted Griffin. While his older brother sounded as if he'd been in a deep sleep, he was happy to let Thane and Finn know to standby.

"I'll follow them from above. If I see anything, I'll try to shift back and call you."

"Good luck."

Because few cars were in the street, he stepped into the middle, shifted, and soared upward. Finding the blue car was easy. They appeared to be heading toward the sea. Some of the coastline was lined with high-end homes overlooking the vast expanse of water, but much of it was desolate because of the ragged cliffs. The Guardians rarely had occasion to go there, so Declan wasn't familiar with all of the terrain.

For the next hour, he followed high above so that neither occupant could detect his shifter signature. He could have cloaked himself, but that would have wasted a lot of energy.

When they arrived at the end of the road, Declan was more confused than ever. There was nothing but black ocean ahead of them. Curious what they were about to do, he cloaked himself and flew toward the sea before swooping downward to investigate.

He couldn't believe these goons. They were climbing aboard a twenty-foot skiff in a rough sea. If they weren't careful, one strong wave would splinter their boat in two. Then Declan would have to save their sorry asses. They started the outboard engine and managed to make it to the open ocean without incident. For the next fifteen minutes, they traveled north along the coast.

Declan spotted the two red lights blinking on the cliff's edge. Sure enough, they headed toward it. It was a cave. Clever. Ten Denlars said that was where the shifters were being held captive. The big question was why there?

Right now, it didn't matter their location. He needed to save these captives. Shit. Even if he incapacitated these two, Declan would need help in rescuing the rest. Before he made the call to Griffin though, he wanted to see what he was up against. As soon as the men moored their boat, they took a motorized inflatable raft into a cove—one that thankfully was rather calm. They pulled to shore—if you could call a two-foot wide beach a shore—and hopped out. Once they secured their small vessel, they climbed a few rocks and entered the cave.

Declan waited a minute before landing. When he did, he had to grip his talons hard to keep from falling. Shifting when he was unsteady was always tricky, but he did it. Once in his human form, it would be easy to follow the two loud mouths.

Given where they were, he changed his mind about looking inside first. Declan pulled out his phone and texted Griffin that the shit was going down. After giving him his coordinates, he asked him to contact Thane and Finn and tell them he needed backup. He pocketed his phone and followed the men inside.

Keeping his distance, he edged his way into the cave wall. Even though periodic red lamps lit the way, his shifter eyesight came in handy. Water ran down the back wall of the very damp cave. He couldn't imagine being trapped in here. He could only hope these shifters were sufficiently drugged or under some spell, making them unaware of their terrible circumstances.

"We can't carry all those cages to the boat," Stick's accomplice whined.

"I only plan to take one of them to show our good faith."

Declan held his breath, waiting to hear who their buyer was. Were the Royals involved or someone else? It was always possible Sanditra had been booted out of the castle after she had failed to turn Kaleena, and then had been unsuccessful with Danita and the other two. If that was true, this might have been her way to get back in their good graces. Too late now though.

Not knowing how long it would take Finn and Thane to arrive, Declan moved closer. He couldn't let these two goons harm any of the shifters.

When Declan finally came to a large opening, he stepped into the main space.

"Hello, boys."

Chapter Twenty-Five

"WHAT THE FUCK are you doing here, Sinclair?" Stick pulled a gun on him.

Declan could shift, as the cave was a good twenty-feet in height, but his ability to maneuver would be somewhat limited. "I came to free the prisoners."

"They aren't prisoners," the associate said. "They're sick animals in need of our care."

That almost made him laugh. Declan waved a hand. "Stick, you might be a vet, but if you haven't noticed, this isn't exactly the most sterile environment. The dampness alone will do more harm than good."

Declan's plan was to stall until reinforcements arrived, but when Stick shifted into a ferocious lion, Declan had no choice but to shift too. He wanted to take the man alive in order to learn as much as he could, but as soon as Stick leapt into the air, Declan was forced to shoot a stream of fire at him. Lion claws could rip his wings to shreds. Without the ability to fly very high inside the cave, avoiding Stick was near to impossible. Yes, he could have cloaked himself, but the end result would be the same—Stick would die.

The lion screamed in agony, and Declan was pissed at himself for having to burn an animal to death, but he'd attacked first.

"Oh, shit. Oh, shit. You fucking killed him." This came from the highly distraught human friend who was still alive.

Not worried about this guy, Declan shifted back and charged toward him. With efficiency, Declan removed the man's gun. Not that a bullet would have been fatal, but it would have stung.

"Declan?" came a call from outside the cave.

"In here, Finn."

Thankfully, Finn, Thane, and Griffin showed up. Thane nodded to the burned shifter. "I take it that was Stick?" he asked.

"Yup."

Thane walked over to the other man who hadn't moved. "We need the key to the cages."

"Stick had it."

The key was now probably bent or, worse, had melted under the intense heat. "We could transport all these cages back to the Four Sisters, I suppose," Declan said, "but it would be far more efficient if one of them could come here to undo the locks and the collars."

"I agree," Finn said. "From the way they all seemed rather lethargic, they might be poisoned like Kaleena and Chelsea had been."

He was certain Chelsea's collar had contained some kind of poison, which made her ability to shift difficult.

"I hate to bother the ladies before dawn, but hopefully, they won't mind."

"I'll head out now," Finn said. "If I have to wait for them to rouse, then I will."

Declan nodded. He pulled out his phone and called his cousin Anderson.

"It's early."

From the grunt that followed, he'd woken him. "It's Declan."

After explaining about locating the ten missing animal shifters, Anderson said he would be there as soon as he could. Dealing with dragon shifters had its advantages.

"What are you going to do with me?" the accomplice asked.

"That's up to the courts to decide. Human trafficking carries a long sentence."

"What are you talking about?"

"You are such a bad liar." Declan faced Thane. "Make sure he doesn't move."

Thane smiled. "My pleasure."

"Griff, help me check out these shifters."

Seven were wolf shifters, two were tramors, and one was a lynx.

"This wolf is in pretty bad shape," Griffin said. "Looks like he put up a good fight."

Declan reached into that cage and placed a healing hand on the wolf's head, and the animal whimpered from his touch. All Declan could think of was Chelsea and what she'd gone through. His mate was one of the strongest people he knew. Closing his eyes, he sent out healing magic. The animal's breaths slowed, and his energy perked up. While Declan could have treated all of them, once their collars were off, he bet most could heal on their own after some much needed rest and proper nutrition.

When Anderson showed up, he escorted the offender out. Because his cousin had flown to the caves, this guy would be treated to a nice flight back. At some point, the cops would have to retrieve the boat and Stick's car. Right now though, this man needed to be interrogated.

Not long after Declan and Griffin made sure the rest of the shifters would survive, Acacia and Primrose arrived. Actually, they materialized next to them. If Declan hadn't expected them to make a grand entrance, he would have been startled.

"Sorry to wake you at this hour, but these men need attention," Declan said.

Primrose waved a hand. "No worries."

Both ladies moved over to the cages. With their back to them, it was hard to see what they were doing, but within seconds, the locks were undone on the cages and the collars removed.

Declan stepped up to the sisters. "Can they shift yet?" he asked.

"Give us a minute."

After some hand waving, humming, and sprinkling of herbs they'd carried with them, three of the men shifted into their human form.

"Where are we?" one of them asked.

Hopefully, Finn, Thane, and Griffin would be willing to fill him in. Declan had a date with a wonderful woman.

CHELSEA SPENT THE first day back on Earth with her very excited parents and siblings, giving them the rundown of her life. Naturally, she told them all about Finn too. Their questions were endless, but she loved how their eyes sparkled when she told them about the dragons and how the Guardians helped protect the realm.

While being back on Earth was wonderful, she missed Declan something fierce. She had hoped that the distance between them would lessen her need, but apparently that hadn't been the case.

"When do you think Declan will return?" her mom asked.

"As soon as he locates the missing shifters that I saw in the back room at the shelter."

"When you came here, was he close to learning their location?"

She didn't want to lie. "No."

Her mom patted her hand. "Your dad and I are happy to see you and to learn about our grandchild. While you're here, you should see a doctor."

Chelsea had thought about that, but she'd find one on Tarradon. "I'm good. Really."

"Suit yourself. What would you like to do today?"

Go home to Tarradon? That thought actually startled her. When had she decided that Earth was no longer her home? Most likely after she had mated with Declan. "I want to catch up on some of my television shows. Being captured took a toll on my body. Not to mention I'm pregnant. Resting sounds wonderful."

Her mom smiled. "Rest it will be. Go into the living room, and I'll bring you some tea."

Chelsea almost cried. She had the best parents in the world. Last night, she'd been surrounded by family and their mates, and it made her homesick for all of them. Today though, she wanted some peace and quiet. Tomorrow, she might go for a run on her old familiar trails.

She had just finished watching the rest of a season of her favorite show when her body vibrated. At first, she thought the baby was acting up, but when the pleasantly erotic sensations increased, she jumped up off the sofa. Declan had to be near.

She was halfway to the front door when a rap sounded. She pulled it open and practically knocked Declan over. He wrapped his arms around her and laughed. Chelsea was so overcome with desire and need that her nails sharpened, blue sparks shot everywhere, and her scales pulsed blue under her skin.

Declan lifted her up and carried her inside. "If anyone saw your skin change colors or mine turn red, there would be too many questions."

Oh, crap. She'd actually forgotten that people on Earth didn't know dragons existed—other than her family, of course. "You're right. Come in."

He set her down. "I can't tell you how excited I am to see you," Declan said.

"I've been dying myself."

"Is that Declan?" her mother called.

"Yes."

Her mom came out of the kitchen, wiping her hands on her apron. "Good to see you Declan. Sort of. I mean you're here to take Chelsea back, I presume."

"Yes."

"We will surely miss her."

Chelsea stepped away from Declan and hugged her mom. "I'll be back. Don't worry."

"Or we can bring you to Tarradon once the baby is born," Declan said.

"Or sooner," Chelsea chimed in.

"Really?" her mother asked.

Her mom might sound excited now, but when the time came, she might chicken out even though Finn and Kaleena had come and gone with no ill effects. "I'd love for you to come and help with the baby," Chelsea said.

"Oh, sweetheart. It's a deal. Can you stay for a bit before you head back?"

Declan nodded. "If you have any of that tea you make, I will."

Mom grinned. "Coming right up."

As soon as she disappeared into the kitchen, Chelsea led Declan into the living room. "I take it you found the shifters?"

"We did." He explained how he'd followed Stick and his associate into some caves. "I wanted Stick alive so I could question him, but he attacked me. I had no choice but to take him out."

"In a way, I'm glad. What he did was really bad."

"The accomplice is in custody, but he's not talking."

She scooted closer to Declan and rubbed her hand down his thigh. That was probably a mistake because she wanted to make love with him really badly. "How are the shifters doing?"

"I left them in the good hands of Primrose and Acacia."

"Did any of them remember what happened?" Chelsea's memory still hadn't fully returned despite Sanditra being dead.

"I didn't question them for long. I was in too big of a hurry to get back to you."

She placed her head on his chest. "Aw. You are so sweet. I've missed you so much."

He turned toward her, lifted her chin, and kissed her.

"Tea anyone?" her mother said with joy.

Chelsea jackknifed up. It was as if she were still in school. "You startled me," Chelsea said.

Her mother just laughed and set the tea in front of them. "How long do you think you can stay?"

Chelsea's eyes widened. "The shelter! I forgot all about it."

"What about it, dear?" her mother asked.

"I just realized that if the owner and his partner are dead, the animals are left unattended."

"Oh, my. That means you have to go, right?"

She looked over at Declan. "Can we go now?"

"Absolutely."

After they finished their tea, they stood. Chelsea's dad came in from outside. "Mom tells me you have to leave?"

She hated to see the disappointment on his face, but she'd be devastated if the animals died because of neglect. "Yes."

She hugged her father and then her mother. "I love you two so much. Mom promised to visit. I hope you can join her too?"

"I'd love that," her dad said.

Knowing that she'd see them again soon, her anxiety level lessened. "Say goodbye to everyone for me."

"We will."

Once outside, Declan pulled out a scale from his pocket. "It's time for you to learn how to make a portal."

"Me?" Chelsea was so excited.

"You're mated to a Guardian. It's time you learn."

"What do I need to do?"

He waved the scale and then handed it to her. "Make a big circle clockwise three times and then two circles counterclockwise. While you are doing that, picture the location of the shelter."

This was exciting and scary at the same time. "What if I mess up?"

Declan laughed. "Then we'll have a long flight ahead of us."

Chapter Twenty-Six

"**I** DID IT!" Chelsea exclaimed.

Most likely, Declan had interfered and guided them to the shelter, but knowing she could move from Earth to Tarradon in a few seconds thrilled her.

Declan wrapped an arm around her waist. "You sure did."

Several of the animals outside barked. "Give me a minute to feed them, okay?"

"That's why we came. I can help too if you tell me what to do."

She so loved him. "How about if I take care of those outside, and you look after the sick ones."

He held up a hand. "I'd like to help, but my magic doesn't extend to animals—only shifters.

She slowly smiled. "If you can shift into a wolf, maybe you inherited some of my other traits. I can heal animals but not humans."

His eyes shone. "If that's the case, perhaps you can heal shifters now too."

Chelsea giggled. "Wouldn't that be fantastic?"

He tapped her butt. "You feed them, and I'll see what I can do to help."

For the next forty-five minutes, Chelsea scurried around to make sure the animals were watered and fed. Tomorrow, she'd return and take them out for their runs. Damn Stick. Why did he have to become involved in something illegal? He'd been a good vet. These animals needed him.

The door to the office opened, and Declan strutted out with a self-satisfied smirk. He tapped his chest. "I am now an even more powerful healer."

She grinned. "What did you do?"

"There was a bird with a fever that I healed."

She rushed over to him and wrapped her arms around his neck. "I hope this doesn't give you a big head. You have enough powers."

"I promise to remain humble." Declan leaned over and kissed her.

Her cells glowed, and her sparks flew. Her need knew no bounds, but making love here was not going to happen. Slightly out of breath, she leaned back. "How about we take this someplace else?"

Declan stroked her face. "Where do you have in mind?"

"Hmm. It's still daylight. I bet the view from on top of the mountain where we first made love would be fantastic."

"It is, but I know of another spot a bit more private with a great view too. It's a twenty-minute flight. You up for it?"

Chelsea reached out and cupped his balls. "If you are."

Declan dropped back his head and laughed. "I'll never be able to thank Fate enough for taking me to you."

"Maybe you'll meet her someday."

His brows furrowed. "On Tarradon, Fate is not a person."

"She is on Earth. Maybe you're wrong, and Fate is a person here too."

He tapped her nose. "Maybe. Ready?"

"You bet."

They both shifted. Declan soared upward, and Chelsea had to work to keep up with him. Finn had told her all about his learning curve when it came to riding the currents and using them to glide, but Chelsea didn't have the luxury of practicing much first.

Declan must have sensed she was working hard, because he slowed down. Instead of coming alongside, he moved in front, and the wind resistance immediately lessened, allowing her to fly using less energy.

Once she wasn't working so hard to fly, Chelsea could enjoy the amazingly lush countryside. Not that Tennessee wasn't a spectacularly beautiful place, it was just that she rarely saw Silver Lake from this kind of vantage point.

The next time she returned to Earth, she'd be sure to stop by and thank Ronan and Blair for needing Declan. If Ronan hadn't had that terrible curse put on him that prevented him from healing, Declan never would have been called down from Tarradon to heal Ronan—and she never would have met her mate.

"See that mountain crest to the east?" Declan telepathed.

"Yes."

"That's where we're going. We'll land on the outskirts of the forest, shift into our wolf form and run in. Needless to say, I've never had the luxury of being in my wolf form there."

Chelsea loved that she could give Declan some of her magic. To think she'd always believed she had gained the most from their mating. It seemed as if he was just as happy.

It wasn't long before he swooped lower, and Chelsea followed him. He found the most perfect spot to touch down. No doubt he probably could have landed on a rock outcropping, but she would have struggled. She needed a lot more practice before she would have her landing legs.

Once on the ground, Chelsea shifted. "That was amazing! I think I'll be spending a lot of my days in the air instead of running in the woods."

Declan moved closer, blue sparks shooting off his body. "Come here, my little fly girl. I can't tell you how thrilled I am that you love to be in the air as much as I do."

"Now how about shifting into your wolf and take me to your den of sin?"

Declan cracked up. "It would be my pleasure. Are you rested enough to keep up?"

She wagged a finger at him. "You never have to worry about me keeping up with you."

"I was talking about racing through the forest."

She shrugged. "That too."

To show him she was at full strength, she shifted. Not knowing the way, she had to let Declan lead. Otherwise, she would have left him in the dust. Running behind him had an advantage in that she could admire his muscular body. He was a combination of black and gray with brown mixed in around his snout. He was truly an impressive animal.

Chelsea had to concede that his strength and stamina was also impressive. After fifteen minutes at a full-out run, she worried a little that she might be too tired for what she had in mind.

They mostly kept to the paths, but at times, he'd cut through the forest, avoiding the switchbacks. Birds chirped, and the sound of a river finally reached her ears. They came to an outcropping of rocks, and Declan slowed in order to squeeze through a small crevice. She couldn't imagine why they had to go to such lengths. Their destination must be spectacular.

When they made it through the narrow confines of the rocks, they were greeted with the most beautiful sight. In front of them was a small lake surrounded by forest. Declan shifted, and Chelsea followed suit.

"Well? It's amazing, isn't it?" Declan asked.

In awe, Chelsea moved next to him. "How did you ever find this place?"

"From flying overhead. I've only been here once, many years ago. You up for a swim?"

She was hot and needed to cool off. "You bet."

Chelsea lifted off her shirt and was about to unhook her bra when she noticed Declan was just standing there. "Are you planning on swimming in your clothes?"

"No, but I don't want to miss seeing you naked. I've missed you so much."

Heat raced up her face. "If you missed me that much, then I hope you'll want to make love with me."

"You know I do."

"Want me to undress you?"

He laughed. "That would end in my dragging you to the ground and having my way with you, and I don't think you'd like me all sweaty."

She planned to be plenty sweaty once they started making love. "Then strip."

As if she'd challenged him to a race, he ditched his shoes, pants, and shirt before she could unhook her bra and step out of her jeans.

Because she was from Tennessee, where the waters were cold much of the year, she ran across the small sandy shore and dove in. When she surfaced, Declan was only up to his ankles.

"Aren't you freezing?" he asked.

"No. I'm used to the cold. If you come here, I'll warm you up."

Declan grinned and dove in. He didn't surface until he'd gathered her in his arms. Naked chest pressed to her breasts, his heat seared her. "Alone at last," he whispered.

"Those are the best words ever," she said.

Chelsea wrapped her legs around his waist, and her pussy went crazy. The lake water shimmered with the light from their blue and red scales. When their lips finally met, she pressed on his shoulders to raise and lower her body, loving how slick she was against his cock.

He slipped his tongue in her mouth, and both of Chelsea's animals fought for a front row seat. Nothing in the world would or could come between them now. Even if a busload of people suddenly appeared on the edge of the lake and started clapping, she wouldn't stop. Her need for him was that great. Maybe it was the fact that the threat against her was gone or that Declan had come out unscathed, but this was where she needed to be.

When he slid his hands down the sides of her body, his thumbs brushed her breasts. She tried to reach his cock, but too many body parts were in the way.

"Let me," he said.

Declan arched his back, reached between them, and deftly slipped his cock straight into her, lighting her up from the inside out.

"I've missed you," she managed to say.

"I've thought of nothing else since I dropped you off at your parents' house. Knowing I could only have you back once I found those shifters made for a powerful and quick search."

She smiled. "I'm glad. Now, kiss me."

"Happy to oblige."

Every thrust of their tongues took her higher and higher. Adding to the immense pleasure was how Declan matched the movements with his thick cock, his strokes strong and urgent. Wanting to participate more fully, she had to dig her fingers into his shoulders for support because he was so slippery.

Declan held her close with one arm while he clutched a handful of hair with the other. They devoured each other with their kisses. Waves lapped around them, and every time he drove into her, he kicked up sand from the lake bottom.

Needing air, she broke the kiss and gulped in oxygen. Her fangs sharpened as did her claws, though she didn't want to look and see if she was more wolf or dragon. Declan's mouth lowered to that delicate spot where her neck met her shoulder, and she found the same place on him.

They both grunted and groaned, clearly trying to hold out for the epic climax that was sure to come. As if they had signaled each other, his fangs sank into her neck at the same time she bit him. The orgasm she'd been holding back burst forth, and she let out a scream. Declan tightened his hold on her and let loose too, his hot seed burning deep inside her. She dropped her head on his shoulder and sagged. A few seconds later, her legs gave way, and she lowered her feet to the bottom.

Holding her chest against his, Declan floated on his back with her on top and slowly kicked his way to shore. It was the best ride ever. When they floated up to within a few feet of the beach, he sat on the sand and lifted her onto his lap.

"Doesn't your cock ever deflate?" she asked for the umpteenth time.

He laughed. "I imagine it will eventually, but not when you're in my arms. I can't help but be ready to go again."

"Give me a minute."

"You can have all the time in the world. No one is around, and I doubt anyone will come here. Think of this as our own private retreat."

She studied him. "Don't tell me you bought this property?"

"No, but I could."

Chelsea smiled. "Good to know."

She leaned her head against his shoulder, content to be in his arms, his comfort erasing the horror of her short captivity. For the rest of her life, she was determined to make Tarradon a better place for her children and all other children.

She lifted her head. "Did I tell you that I love you?"

"Hmm." He dragged a hand down his chin. "Can't say that you've ever have."

She laughed. "Then I guess I know what I'll be doing from now on."

"And I'll do the same. Have you recovered yet from your swim?"

"Yes."

Declan slipped her off his lap and leaned her back, making sure that her head rested on the grassy edge. "I'm hungry again. For you."

With that he began his feast, and Chelsea was sure nothing would surpass it. Life with Declan Sinclair would be wonderful. Not only was he the noblest of shifters, he would make the absolute best father.

Don't forget to sign up for my newsletter *to receive three free books, as well as up-to-date information on my stories. If you prefer to only receive notices regarding my releases, follow me on BookBub.*

I hope you enjoyed Chelsea and Declan's story. Next up is Angelique and Thane's story, called PASSIONATE FLAMES.

Here is the first chapter:

"YOU'RE PREGNANT?" Angelique Carson asked with as much surprise as she could pull off. Given her whole being was created in order to watch over the children of the Guardians, she'd been well aware of her friend's condition for a while. First came Chelsea McKinnon, who would bear a child in about six months, and now Kaleena Sinclair.

"I just found out!"

"How far along are you?"

Kaleena placed a hand on her stomach. "Two months."

Angelique smiled. "What an exciting time for you." She waved for one of the servers in her coffee shop to come over.

Shannon rushed to their table. "What can I get you?"

"Can you bring us two coffees?" Angelique asked. "We need to celebrate."

"Absolutely," her second in command said with a smile.

Not only did she want to celebrate, Angelique also wanted to spend a bit more time with her best friend. Kaleena was always working and never took enough time for herself. Now more than ever, she needed to learn to relax.

"Make mine a tea," Kaleena said. Shannon nodded and hurried off. "Finn keeps telling me all of his Earth stories about how bad caffeine is for the baby."

Angelique smiled. From what she'd been told, that wasn't the case on Tarradon, but she didn't feel it was her place to say anything.

"I'm surprised you left work in the middle of the day, but I'm glad you stopped by. I've missed our chats." Kaleena never played hooky.

She sighed. "Normally, I wouldn't have left, but Finn made me promise to ask if you would put a protective sac around our baby—like the one you did for Chelsea. Even though I won't be entering into any dragon battles any time soon, Finn, as well as many of my family members, is worried that something might come up where I'll be forced to fight. He wants our child to be safe."

So did she. "I totally understand."

Kaleena leaned forward. "I'll admit it bugs me they think just because I'm pregnant that I'm helpless. I'm not. I can defend myself. I've proved that time and time again. I so want to fly and engage in a little sparring." She glanced at the ceiling. "Doing battle invigorates me."

Angelique loved her friend's passion but not her decision to act recklessly, especially now. "I can teach you some meditation that will keep the baby safe once I put the protective spell on your child. I can also guide you on to how to fight safely should the need arise."

Kaleena reached across the table and grasped Angelique's hand. "Really? But you're not a shifter."

"I know, but I've been watching fights for a while now." She winked.

Kaleena's shoulders relaxed. "You're the best. When can we get together? I can train whenever you are free."

"How about tomorrow around five? Melissa and Shannon can run the coffee shop without me for a few hours."

"Fantastic."

They discussed where to meet and decided the Sinclair Mines would provide a place where Angelique could work in private to keep the baby safe as well as show Kaleena some safe flying techniques in the large field behind the main offices.

They chatted a bit about how things were going with Angelique's new coffee shop and what else she was up to. "Basically, things have been great. Life has been calm since the incident with Chelsea,"

Angelique said. "That was the last real adrenaline rush I've had. Ever since then it's been business as usual."

"That was an adventure—or rather a painful misadventure. I can't tell you how much better I feel knowing that bitch Sanditra is dead. She nearly ruined my life."

Angelique held up a finger. "As horrible as your incarceration was, if it hadn't been for that dark lighter, Finn might not have traveled from Earth to Tarradon to save you, which means you still might not be with your mate."

Kaleena chuckled. "There is that."

Their second round of drinks arrived, and they chatted about Kaleena's family for a bit. Angelique noticed that her friend brought up her brother Thane's name a lot. Yes, whimsical Fate had decided now that Angelique was in this human form, she should have a mate, and that mate was Thane, but it was hard not to let on that she knew.

There was no denying that the man was gorgeous, powerful, and highly driven, but Angelique's main job on Tarradon was to protect the progeny of Guardians—not have hot sex all day long. When all of the Sinclair and Caspian children were grown, she'd focus on her own pleasure.

Shattering dishes broke their intimate conversation. "Really? I guess I should deal with that. Drinks are on the house," Angelique said as she scooted out of the booth. "Tomorrow at the mine at five."

Kaleena smiled. "See you then. And thank you."

Angelique went about her business, while Kaleena finished her drink before leaving. Even though running the coffee shop gave her something to do while she waited for Chelsea's and now Kaleena's baby to arrive, Angelique loved this place. It gave her a chance to talk to people all day long, which was something she sorely missed when she was a white light entity in another realm.

THE DELIVERY OF the wood Thane Sinclair had ordered for the obstacle course he was building behind the mine was delayed until tomorrow morning. Crap. He already had delayed all training with the Guardians or anyone else for that matter in order to complete the course. This delay put a further kink in his plans. He needed this last piece to be finished before he could return to his fitness center in town.

Now that he had some free time, he stopped by his family's mining office to see if anyone could use his help. They often asked him to run down delinquent accounts because after one look at his muscular body, the mining businessmen usually paid up pronto. He never had to threaten anyone with violence—not that he would—because the Sinclair name and his apparent fierce look were enough to squeeze the last dollar out of a person.

Thane entered the office and looked to see who was there. Declan's office was empty, but Finn McKinnon was there. He knocked on his door and entered.

"Hey," Finn said. "How's the obstacle course coming? You finish it yet?"

Thane explained about the delay. "Because of that, I have some time and wondered if you needed a hand."

Finn's brows rose. "As a matter of fact, I was just about to call you."

He hadn't expected that. "About what?"

"I have some good news."

Thane could use some of that. He pulled up a chair and faced Finn's desk. "What is it?"

"I am going to be a dad. We just found out that Kaleena is two months pregnant!"

Thane reached out and pumped Finn's extended fist. "Awesome, man. That's so exciting. Uncle Thane has a nice ring to it." Actually, Kaleena told him two days ago but made him promise not to let on that he knew.

"It is, but the bad news is that my stubborn mate refuses to slow down. She sees no reason not to engage in battle should the Guardians need her."

Thane almost chuckled. "My sister always was stubborn. When she comes for her usual training I'll make sure to take it easy."

Finn shook his head. "You know that no matter what you say, she'll work twice as hard as before to prove to you that she will always be ready—baby or not."

What Finn said was true. Thane leaned back in his chair. "Then I'll ask her to stop by here tomorrow for some special training. That way she won't have anyone to compete against. I'll do some research on how she can protect her child while she executes the maneuvers. You know as well as I that neither Declan nor Dad would ever put her in the field now."

Finn blew out a breath. "Neither will I, but sometimes she doesn't listen to anyone. Can you text her with a time and place? She'll think I'm just an over protective mate if I deliver the message."

Thane smiled. "Can do."

He couldn't be more pleased that his sister was having a baby. That would make two new little Sinclair Guardians ready to greet the world. A twang of jealousy surfaced at that thought. He'd always wanted a child, but considering how Angelique always ended their far and few between dates with a chaste kiss, he wouldn't be mating with her anytime soon.

To avoid what little relationship they had between them, he'd stopped being near her. He just couldn't handle it. His dragon kept breathing fire inside his gut from wanting her so much. After he'd fought Sanditra, Angelique had brought him back from the brink of death. From that moment on, his need for her had grown to the point of distraction.

"Later, Finn."

Thane left his office and headed home. After doing a bit of research on how to protect a pregnant dragon during battle, Thane contacted Kaleena and told her Finn had let the cat out of the bag.

"I want to go over some fighting techniques that will keep you and the baby safe."

"Thank you, but everyone is way over protective. It's not like I'm the first dragon to have a child."

He almost smiled at her defiance. "True. Can you meet me at the Sinclair Mine tomorrow at five? I want to have a one-to-one with you. Onlookers tend to distract."

She hesitated for a moment, and then practically giggled. "That's perfect timing!"

In all honesty, Thane thought Kaleena would balk at having to tone down her training. He was just pleased he'd dodged an argument.

Assuming the wood he needed would be delivered tomorrow morning as promised, he would be at the mines all day working on the final stages of building the obstacle course. Having her come to the mines around five would be ideal.

In need of some relaxation after the mess up with the material delivery, Thane headed over to the Wing's Bar. He loved they had a flat roof on which to land, along with a stairwell that exited out to the back of the bar. Not that all of the customers were dragon shifters, but the majority were. Since parking around the bar was a bitch, flying was much easier.

Tonight was Finn's night off to bartend, so Thane ordered his scotch from Barry who unfortunately wasn't as generous with the whiskey as Finn. Once Barry delivered his drink, Thane spun around on his bar stool to watch the patrons. People watching was one of his favorite pastimes.

Halfway into his drink, his skin prickled and his gold scales flickered under his skin. Shit. Here he thought he'd have a nice relaxing evening. Nope. Angelique had to show up, messing with his libido something fierce. While he always enjoyed watching his beautiful mate, when she acted as if he wasn't anything special, it drove him crazy. She might only be a white lighter and not a shifter, but even she'd admitted one night that they were mates. Why she wouldn't do anything about it was anyone's guess. Hell, he could see from the way her eyes sparkled and her skin pulsed white that she wanted him. Something was holding her back, only she refused to tell him what it was. But Thane Sinclair wasn't a Guardian for nothing. He'd find out one way or the other.

Laughter floated his way. When he spotted his fair-haired beauty, his pulse soared once more. Thane waited for Angelique to turn toward him and at least wave, but instead she wove her way down the aisle between the tables, smiling at two of her friends. One of the women with her was Melissa, but he couldn't remember the other one's name. Both, however, worked at her coffee shop.

He chugged the rest of his drink. While Thane should probably leave, he wasn't ready. Just because the woman who made his scales glow and his cock hard had entered the bar, it didn't mean he should cut short his relaxation time.

Soon, this teasing affair had to end though. Angelique was his mate, and he was determined to win her over.

"THANE'S STARING AT you again," Melissa said with too much glee.

"Is that so?" Angelique said, attempting to act nonchalant. She never should have sat in the booth facing him, but she couldn't help it. Thane was hot, especially with his tanned skin, short dark hair, and square jaw—not to mention those piercing green eyes.

Angelique probably should give some excuse to leave, but she'd asked her two employees out for a drink to celebrate the half-year anniversary of the opening of Angelique's Coffee Shop, and she'd be damned if Thane Sinclair was going to ruin it.

"Hey, if you don't want him, would you mind if I give him a shot?" Melissa asked.

An unexpected and unwanted surge of lust slammed into her that she refused to call jealousy. Sure, they were mates, but Fate never said she needed to do anything about it right away. Angelique would have urged Melissa to have a go at him, but her friend would only be disappointed when she found out nothing could come from it. Thane seemed to have his sights on Angelique, and she suspected no other woman would be able to change his mind. "I heard he's engaged or something."

Melissa's eyes widened. "Really? You'd never know it. I've never seen him with anyone. Remember, when he used to come into the coffee shop when we first opened?"

How could she not? Her white light had pulsed from the inside out. "I recall him coming in a few times."

"He was always alone. If he has a lady friend, where is she?"

"Next time we chat, I'll ask him." Angelique smiled. As if some guardian angel was watching, a server rushed over to take their drink orders.

Angelique looked at her two friends. "How about we split a pitcher of Sangria?"

Before Finn arrived from Earth, the drink didn't exist. He'd introduced Edendale to the delicious concoction, and it was a big hit at the bar.

"I'm game," Shannon said.

"Me too," Melissa chimed in.

Their server said he'd be right back.

Angelique had been looking forward to tonight, but maybe it had been a mistake to come to the one place Thane often frequented. After Kaleena had talked about how Thane had been building some huge obstacle course, her imagination had gone wild thinking about what his calloused palms could do to her body. She hated when she let her imagination run wild, but somehow she was powerless to stop herself from thinking about him. Had she known he'd be there tonight, she might have suggested a different location.

Or… had she secretly wanted to run into him? Sheesh. She was slowly falling apart with indecision, which wasn't good on any level. At some point, she just might have to jump his bones to get him out of her system. Fate had been cruel in giving her two tasks: ensure the safety of the Guardian children and deal with a mate. One or the other she could handle. Both at the same time was just too much.

"Why don't you go over there and talk to him?" Shannon urged. "I swear I saw his arms pulse gold when he looked at you. He wants you." She sighed. "I bet he is as beautiful a dragon as he is a man."

Angelique never should have told these humans that Thane was a shifter, but when they'd asked for details about how she had helped save Chelsea from the dark lighter, she had to give them some information.

"Thane Sinclair is a warrior. He spends his whole life training people to fight. He's just not my type." She hoped no darkness started to grow inside her from that lie.

In truth, growing up Angelique never believed it was possible for her to have a mate given she was pure light, but once she saw Thane, she understood why Fate had paired him with her. Her purpose in life had always been to help people from afar. It wasn't until she was called to this realm that she'd even had a body. Too bad, it had to be one that was sensitive to a man's touch—or rather to Thane's touch.

When Angelique had first shown up in Thedia province, it had taken her months to learn how to interact with people effectively. She had to learn which people were good and which ones were bad, but when she did help them, it had been a rush.

To fully understand what humans and shifters were thinking and how and why they reacted the way they did, she'd engaged in many activities—the most pleasurable of which was sex. Even though it was nice, she was a bit disappointed that the world didn't stand still as so many had claimed it would—that was until she came near Thane. No, they'd not engaged in that carnal pleasure—and wouldn't be a long time—but the few little kisses she'd had when he said goodnight had done more to stimulate her than any full-blown encounter ever had.

She almost smiled at the memory of how her body had screamed *mate-mate* as soon as she met him. Finding Thane so soon after her arrival to this realm had been a shock, but there was nothing wrong with waiting a few hundred more years—assuming she could hold out that long.

HIDDEN REALMS OF SILVER LAKE (Paranormal)

Awakened By Flames (book 1)

Seduced By Flames (book 2)

Kissed By Flames (book 3)

Destiny In Flames (book 4)

Passionate Flames (book 5)

WERES & WITCHES OF SILVER LAKE

A Magical Shift (book 1) – FREE

Catching Her Bear (book 2)

Surge of Magic (book 3)

The Bear's Forbidden Wolf (book 4)

Her Reluctant Bear (book 5)

Freeing His Tiger (book 6)

Protecting His Wolf (book 7)

Waking His Bear (book 8)

Melting Her Wolf's Heart (book 9)

Her Wolf's Guarded Heart (book 10)

His Rogue Bear (book 11)

PACK WARS (Paranormal)

Training Their Mate (book 1) – FREE

Claiming Their Mate (book 2)

Rescuing Their Virgin Mate (book 3)

Loving Their Vixen Mate (book 4)

Fighting For Their Mate (book 5)

Enticing Their Mate (book 6)

Boxed Set (books 1-3)

Boxed Set (books 1-4)

Complete Box Set (books 1–6)

MONTANA PROMISES (Full length contemporary)
Promises of Mercy (book 1)
Foundations For Three (book 2)
Montana Fire (book 3)
Montana Promises Box Set (books 1-3)
Hart To Hart (book 4)
Burning Seduction (book 5)
Montana Promises Complete Box Set (books 1–5)

ROCK HARD, MONTANA (contemporary novellas)
Montana Desire (book 1)
Awakening Passions (book 2)

PLEDGED TO PROTECT (contemporary romantic suspense)
Panic and Passion (book 1)
Danger and Desire (book 2)
Terror and Temptation (book 3)
Pledged To Protect Box Set (books 1–3)

HIDDEN HILLS SHIFTERS (Paranormal)
An Unexpected Diversion (book 1) – FREE
Bare Instincts (book 2)
Shifting Destinies (book 3)
Box Set (books 1–3)
Embracing Fate (book 4)
Promises Unbroken (book 5)
Bear 'N Dirty (book 6)
Hidden Hills Shifters Complete Box Set

A NASH MYSTERY (Contemporary)
Sidearms and Silk (book 1)
Black Ops and Lingerie (book 2)

Author Bio

Want 3 FREE books? Sign up for my newsletter.

COPY AND PASTE INTO YOUR BROWSER:
smarturl.it/o4cz93?IQid=MLite

Check out my latest interview on You Tube:
youtube.com/watch?v=sQo5pyyVMDI

Not only do I love to read, write, and dream, I'm an extrovert. I enjoy being around people and am always trying to understand what makes them tick. Not only must my books have a happily ever after, I need characters I can relate to. My men are wonderful, dynamic, smart, strong, and the best lovers in the world (of course).

I believe I am the luckiest woman. I do what I love and I have a wonderful, supportive husband, who happens to be hot!

Fun facts about me

(1) I'm a math nerd who loves spreadsheets. Give me numbers and I'll find a pattern.

(2) I love photography, so I'll be posting pictures—especially of my Costa Rican adventure.

(3) I also like to exercise. Yes, I know I'm odd. Not only do I lift weights, I love to hike and walk on the beach (yes, it sounds like an ad for a date).

I love hearing from readers either on FB or via email (hint, hint).

Social Media Sites

Website:
www.velladay.com

FB:
facebook.com/vella.day.90

Twitter:
@velladay4

Gmail:
velladayauthor@gmail.com

Google:
plus.google.com/u/0/116041077486216602121/posts

Instagram:
@dayvella

www.ingramcontent.com/pod-product-compliance
Lightning Source LLC
Chambersburg PA
CBHW020944180626
46814CB00003B/927